THE SECRET OF
STONESHIP WOODS

READ ALL THE

SPY GEAR

ADVENTURES

ADVENTURES

THE SECRET OF STONESHIP WOODS

BY RICK BARBA

SCHOLASTIC INC.
New York Toronto London Auckland Sydney
Mexico City New Delhi Hong Kong Buenos Aires

ISBN-13: 978-0-439-02486-0
ISBN-10: 0-439-02486-2

Text copyright © 2006 by Wild Planet Toys, Inc.
Illustrations copyright © 2006 by Scott Fischer.
Map of Carrolton copyright © 2006 by Eve Steccati. All rights reserved.
Published by Scholastic Inc., 557 Broadway, New York, NY 10012, by arrangement with Aladdin Paperbacks, an imprint of Simon & Schuster Children's Publishing Division.
Spy Gear and Wild Planet trademarks are the property of Wild Planet Toys, Inc., San Francisco, CA 94104. SCHOLASTIC and associated logos are trademarks and/or registered trademarks of Scholastic Inc.

12 11 10 9 8 7 6 5 4 3 2   7 8 9 10 11 12/0

Printed in the U.S.A.   40

First Scholastic printing, January 2007

Designed by Tom Daly

The text of this book was set in Weiss.

CONTENTS

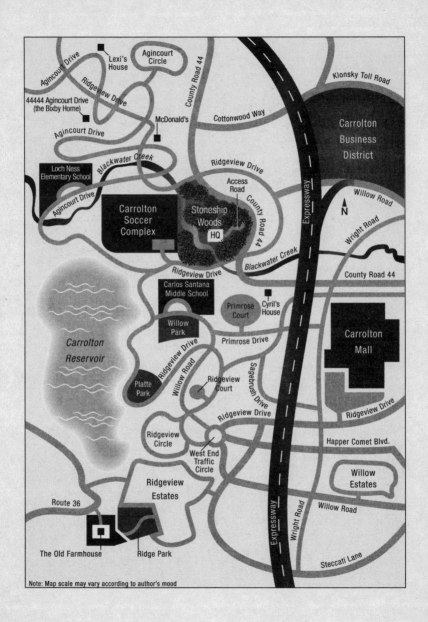

Lexi's House

Agincourt Circle

Agincourt Drive

Ridgeview Drive

County Road 44

Klonsky Toll Road

44444 Agincourt Drive (the Bixby Home)

McDonald's

Cottonwood Way

Agincourt Drive

Carrolton Business District

Blackwater Creek

Ridgeview Drive

Loch Ness Elementary School

Access Road

Willow Road

Agincourt Drive

Carrolton Soccer Complex

Stoneship Woods

HQ

County Road 44

N

Wright Road

Blackwater Creek

Ridgeview Drive

County Road 44

Carlos Santana Middle School

Primrose Court

Cyril's House

Carrolton Reservoir

Willow Park

Primrose Drive

Carrolton Mall

Ridgeview Drive

Platte Park

Willow Road

Ridgeview Court

Sagebrush Drive

Ridgeview Drive

Ridgeview Circle

Ridgeview Drive

Happer Comet Blvd.

Route 36

West End Traffic Circle

Willow Estates

Ridgeview Estates

Expressway

Wright Road

Willow Road

The Old Farmhouse

Ridge Park

Steccati Lane

Note: Map scale may vary according to author's mood

TEAM SPY GEAR

 JAKE BIXBY

 LUCAS BIXBY

 CYRIL WONG

 LEXI LOPEZ

WELCOME TO CARROLTON

Pretend you're a spy satellite.

Look down at the Earth. Your eye is a telescope with amazing powers of magnification. You can see the ant on a log near Lake Superior—no, not that black ant. The red ant over there! See it? The one leading a column of red ants, preparing to crush the black ant colony? It will be a gruesome battle, with much shredding of ant flesh, so maybe you shouldn't watch. Anyway, you're too close. Pull back, will you?

Okay, that's better.

See that town over there—the one with all the malls and multiplex cinemas and the suburban streets twisted like pretzels to discourage "through traffic"?

That's Carrolton, the home of the Bixby family.

See the man sleeping in that blue Toyota over on

Primrose Drive? That's Mr. Latimer. He's been lost in the subdivision for almost three years now. Fortunately, the neighborhood has taken him in—feeding him, letting him use their "facilities" (you know what that means), and occasionally giving out directions that make Mr. Latimer even more confused and lost. The poor man just wants to find the Expressway.

Now swivel your spy telescope to the Bixby house at 44444 Agincourt Drive. Look carefully for the exact address, because these are "custom homes." That means they've been carefully designed to look exactly the same, even though they're actually different houses. (This requires a great degree of skill and craftsmanship.) Did you find 44444 Agincourt Drive yet? Keep looking. This may take a few weeks, but don't give up.

Ah, there it is.

That faux colonial house (*faux* means "actually, it's fake") is the Bixby home. Zoom right through the family room window. No, not that one! That's the bathroom! Don't look in there, for gosh sakes! Try the window just to the left.

Yes, that's it. *That's* the Bixby family room.

Spies live here. Two of them, in fact. Can you believe it? Spies with amazing spy gadgets that let them listen through walls and see clearly in the darkest nights. But here's the amazing thing. These spies are less than four-teen years old! And what's more, the two young spies who live at 44444 Agincourt Drive are probably the best spies in the world.

Anyway, these two world-class spies live in a happy neighborhood where nothing much goes wrong. Carrolton parents work very, very hard. They make sure their children are much too busy to get in trouble. Yes, Carrolton is a happy, busy place. But elsewhere, things are horribly wrong. Evil lurks on the outskirts. Evil that must be watched.

This, of course, is the purpose of spying—to keep an eye on the bad guys.

Jake and Lucas Bixby are brothers.

Brothers are special people. Oh sure, they fight and kick each other sometimes—sometimes right in the butt, if you must know. Brothers often yell and poke and call each other names that only U.S. Marines fully understand. They can be *rambunctious*, a word that makes me laugh every time I try to say it with a straight face.

But enough about me. The Bixby brothers are different from other brothers, and that's what this book is about: the Bixby brothers. Well, it's about espionage and mayhem and conspiracy and murky enemies too. But let's start at the beginning. Let's look at the origins of Team Spy Gear, which is of course part of the title of the book, so you knew it had to be coming.

It all starts with the Bixby boys.

(2)

MEET THE BIXBYS

That boy doing push-ups on the family room floor is Jake Bixby, thirteen.

Why is Jake doing push-ups? Because the Bixbys are playing one of their favorite games, Monopoly: The Fitness Edition.

Mr. Bixby, Jake's father, a tall corporate executive with perfect blond hair, leans away from the board and talks on his cell phone. Oops, now he's yelling. Let's move away from him, shall we? Quickly, let's go over by Mrs. Bixby, a very short school counselor with dark hair and nice skin. She's counting Jake's push-ups to make sure he doesn't cheat.

"You're bending at the waist, honey," she says.

"Sorry."

"Keep your butt down."

"Mom!"

"Those last two don't count."

"Okay," says Jake. "I'll do two extra."

Maybe we should move away from Mrs. Bixby, too. After all, she's the kind of woman who gets very angry if people proceed out of turn at a four-way stop. Mr. Bixby, on the other hand, is the kind of man who discusses business with somebody named Chad during a family round of Monopoly. Then again, Mrs. Bixby is the kind of woman who schedules family rounds of Monopoly, marking the start time on her digital calendar.

But enough about parents. Parents, after all, can be very boring.

Look at Jake. Look closely.

He's an average-size, average-looking kid. Brown hair, brown eyes. But guess what? He's not average. In fact there's something oddly special about Jake Bixby—let's call it an aura—almost as if he was destined for greatness. Okay, maybe he's not exactly Luke Skywalker or Harry Potter. But he's special. For example, Jake loves his parents, despite their flaws. That's a sign of greatness if ever there was one.

And here's another: Jake refuses to let his boxers stick out of his pants.

Suddenly the lights go out.

"Lucas!" shout Mr. and Mrs. Bixby in unison.

Jake grins. (Note: Jake's the kind of kid who "grins" instead of "smiles.") Lucas is Jake's younger brother, an eleven-year-old with far too much energy and a burning curiosity about how stuff works. Mechanical stuff, electronic stuff—gadgets, devices, you name it.

The lights go back on.

"Sorry," calls Lucas from the kitchen.

"Lucas, what's that bad sound?" Mrs. Bixby says with alarm.

"Uh, the microwave."

"What's it doing?"

"Making ice."

Lucas Bixby enters the family room. He is a skinny, black-haired kid with huge green eyes. He does everything with gusto. He moves *way* too fast. He spills his milk almost daily. When he chews gum, it sounds like slime creatures are attacking from multiple directions. You know the type.

"Is it my turn yet?"

"Yes, as soon as your brother stops cheating."

Lucas laughs. The thought of Jake cheating is quite amusing. He rolls the dice.

"Six!" he shouts.

He moves his Monopoly piece (a barbell) six spaces, slamming the board at each space. The entire Monopoly world suffers tremors of magnitude 6.8.

"Ha *ha!*" shrieks Lucas. "Triathlon Avenue! I'll buy that asset!"

"What's the rent?" asks Mrs. Bixby, peering over her

glasses as she plucks the Triathlon Avenue property card out of a stack.

"Take a guess."

Jake groans and stands. "I'll get the bike."

Well, now you know the Bixbys.

But we have more people to meet.

Suddenly a loud noise from upstairs stops the game. All Bixby eyes turn to the staircase. A few more bangs resound from the upper hallway. Then Lexi Lopez, eleven, neighbor and best friend of Lucas, skips down the steps.

"Dude!" says Lucas, surprised.

"Dude," says Lexi. They do their special handshake. It ends with a slap of palms and a knuckle punch.

Lucas says, "How'd you get upstairs?"

"I crawled in your bedroom window," says Lexi. She shrugs. "It was open."

"But how?"

"I climbed the drainpipe."

"Mad skills!" says Lucas with admiration. They shake again. "So that gymnastics class your mom makes you take is doing some good."

"I guess."

"I thought you were taking ballet, Lexi," says Mrs. Bixby as she studies the game board and punches some keys on her calculator.

"That too."

"That's *so* sad," says Lucas.

Jake nods hello and says, "Yo, Lexi, what's up with your face?"

Lexi sits next to Lucas and touches her scraped cheek.

"You need to fix your drainpipe," she says.

Now the doorbell rings.

"I'll get it," says Jake.

Cyril Wong, thirteen, Jake's best friend in the world, stands on the front porch. He's tall, goofy, smart, gawky, and has the worst-looking hair of anybody west of the Dardanelles, a strait in northwest Turkey connecting the Sea of Marmara with the Aegean. In fact, if you were a mean kid, you might call Cyril a name like "mop head" in a mean way.

"Yo, mop head," says Jake, but not in a mean way.

"'Sup?" says Cyril.

"Same ol'," says Jake.

"Word," nods Cyril, hair flopping.

They slap hands and walk into the family room.

Mrs. Bixby has just about had it with these blessed interruptions. Her Monopoly timetable has been ruined. She gets up and says, "I *really* expected to be in the latter stages of the game by now."

"Sorry, Mom," says Jake.

"Gosh, I'm sorry, Mrs. Bixby," says Cyril.

"Those numbers don't add up, Chad!" yells Mr. Bixby

at his cell phone. He glares at it, as if the phone itself is named Chad.

Mrs. Bixby looks at her husband and says, "Tell your father that I'm in the *kitchen* again." Her voice sounds like the kind of icicles that hang from the rusty tailpipe of a bad car.

She leaves the room.

Cyril watches her go, then looks at Jake. "Not good," he says.

"Why do you say that?"

"Well, her voice."

"What about it?"

"She *slays* things with it," says Cyril. "My mom does that too." He tries to run his fingers through his hair, but fails. Then he adds: "Moms can, like, crush trucks with their words."

Jake nods, because this is true. Too bad moms forget about this chilling power sometimes. Dads too, of course.

Then Cyril gives Jake a look.

He glances at Lucas and Lexi, too.

They all know each other very well, these four—*so* well that words are sometimes unnecessary. Jake, Lucas, and Lexi all stand up. They know that Cyril's look means something like this: *Very interesting and possibly disturbing information has emerged from the data I'm scanning at Stoneship, so let's hurry back to HQ, shall we?*

Jake claps Cyril on the shoulder.

Lexi and Lucas exchange a meaningful look that only grizzled spies understand.

The Bixby boys nod at each other in a brotherly way.

Then Jake heads for the front door.

The others follow.

This looks like a job for . . . *Team Spy Gear*!

Hey, wait a minute.

What *is* Stoneship? You don't even know yet, do you? Plus we said we'd investigate the origins of Team Spy Gear, didn't we?

Well, by golly, we meant it. So let's go back to a time in the past. Let's go back to a time months before, predating now . . . back, back to a time when Team Spy Gear was still in the future and "back then" was actually "now" and the real "now," which of course is The Present, was yet to come.

Wait. Could you read the previous sentence again?

If you understand it, please write and explain it to me, because after writing it, I have no idea where we are now.

A COMPLEX GLIMPSE

It was a typical day at the Carrolton Soccer Complex, not long ago.

Jake Bixby juggled a soccer ball on the fenced-in Juggling Green, waiting for the trolley to arrive. His parents stood nearby, talking on their cell phones. In the trolley station, Lucas Bixby jotted on a pad. He was diagramming the track-switch mechanism that directed trolley cars down three crisscrossing routes through the 257-acre complex.

Today Jake's game was scheduled on Field 51—only a twelve-minute ride, with no transfers! But his team was playing the Crush Diamond, a team sponsored by several Wall Street banking firms and loaded with the biggest thirteen-year-olds money could buy.

Jake fully expected to be maimed. But he always

played hard. He knew how important "playing hard" was to his parents.

"Just do your best, honey," his mom would say. "That's all we ask. Just your most excellent best, is all. Just try your hardest, expending all your sweat and blood and energy, because 100 percent effort is its own reward, in terms of satisfaction."

"Okay, Mom."

"And play fair, Son," his dad would add.

"Yes, sir."

"If somebody fouls you, it's totally fair to kick them really hard," Mr. Bixby would add, pointing at his leg, "like right here, this spot on the bone where shinguards don't cover."

"Dad—"

"And you know, Son, I'd retaliate when the center referee isn't looking—which is pretty much most of the time, it seems to me. These guys are idiots, aren't they? Where do the referee assignors find such lowly primates?"

"They do their best, Dad."

"Their best?"

Mr. Bixby would laugh really hard at that one.

The Soccer Complex was located just a few blocks south of the Bixbys' neighborhood, so the family would walk together to games. For Jake, nothing was better. Walking together as a family, his parents holding hands— every week! As Jake juggled the ball, he thought about how good this life was. He didn't mind getting annihilated every weekend by teams named Storm and Arsenal and Crush and Repress, as long as the Bixbys were together.

"Jake! Jake!"

Jake looked up. Cyril was running toward him, his hair flouncing like a shrub in a hurricane.

"Hey man!"

Cyril tried to jump over the low fence. But his foot caught the fence top and he executed a full forward roll. The rubbery sound of human flesh smacking the ground could be heard for miles, but then Cyril popped up and continued running, as if the entire move was planned from the start, perhaps even weeks ago.

Cyril's run was a thing of beauty, too. It looked like he had several extra arms. Jake shook his head in mute admiration. His best buddy was amazing, a one-of-a-kind specimen, plus he was doggedly loyal. And that was another thing to be grateful for on this beautiful day. Jake grinned (there he goes again! grinning!) knowing that it would be easy to lose count if he tried to count his blessings.

The boys slapped hands.

"Whew! Made it!" said Cyril. "Still alive!"

"Dude," said Jake. "You *arrive* like nobody I know."

"Thanks, man."

Clanging bells announced the imminent departure of a trolley. Jake picked up his soccer ball.

"You do know we play the Crush today," he said.

"Yes," said Cyril. "That's why I brought my lucky hat."

He pulled a cap out of his pocket and tried to cram it over his hair. The result looked like somebody driving a fist into a huge feather pillow. When Jake saw the cap, he started laughing. It read CRUSH SOCCER CLUB with the Crush logo.

"Thanks for the support," said Jake.

"Hey, you don't know what it's like in the bleachers," said Cyril.

"It's bad?"

"It's murder, man." Cyril struck a pose that resembled one of those little soccer guys on the tops of trophies. He added, "I also brought morphine and some IV tubes."

"Excellent."

Clang! Clang! The trolley was ready to go.

The four Bixbys and Cyril hopped aboard.

Field 51 spread like a perfect carpet along the east edge of the Soccer Complex.

It bordered the only unincorporated strip of land in all of Carrolton—a wild, dark patch of snaggly bushes and towering trees. People called it "Stoneship Woods," though nobody knew why. Nobody went in there. Kids said it was haunted, or maybe just infested with wild insects that would eat your eye jelly.

Lucas Bixby stared at the dense foliage. It looked impenetrable.

"Dude!" called a voice.

Lucas turned to see Lexi jogging toward him from the next field. Lexi wore a soccer uniform so elaborate it could have been designed by French fashion experts.

"Yo dog!" said Lucas. They did their handshake. "When do you play?"

"Just did," said Lexi, looking uncomfortable.

"Uh-oh." Lucas noted Lexi's evasive eyes. "Who?"

Lexi said, "Um, Crush U-12, their, uh, developmental squad."

"Developmental?" asked Lucas.

"So they say."

Developmental leagues are supposed to consist of "recreational" teams full of happy young kids preparing for play in competitive divisions. In the case of the Crush Soccer Club, "developmental" meant "future members of Navy SEAL Team Bravo." Most Crush teams had a coaching staff of eight, plus a full-time recruiter.

"Well, you survived," said Lucas.

"I didn't play."

"No? Why not?"

"I cried too much."

Lucas nodded. "Good tactic."

The two buddies kicked Lexi's soccer ball back and forth. Out on the field Jake's team was wilting under the relentless attack of the Crush cyborgs. On the far sideline Crush parents cheered goal after goal, while the Crush team lawyer tactfully pointed out officiating errors. Cyril came over and joined the younger kids.

"I just can't watch anymore," he said.

"It's grisly," agreed Lucas.

"Kick it here."

Lexi tapped the ball over to Cyril.

Then something caught Cyril's eye. He said, "Hey, what's that?"

I don't want to give too much away, but are you paying attention? This may not *seem* like a big moment, but it is. Trust me. You may even want to whip out a highlighter and mark this passage.

"Where?" said Lucas.

"There, in the trees," said Cyril.

Lexi and Lucas peered into Stoneship Woods where Cyril pointed. The wind lifted some branches, revealing a swatch of something gray and solid in the wild tangle of foliage.

"Looks like concrete," said Cyril.

"Or a wall," said Lexi.

"What do you suppose it is?" asked Lucas.

"A concrete wall?" suggested Lexi.

"My guess is a secret military installation," said Cyril. "That might be the lab where they do the UFO autopsies. See, they extract the alien DNA and implant it in human subjects, who breed and then their offspring join the Crush Soccer Club."

Lexi and Lucas both looked at Cyril.

"It's documented," he said.

Lucas suddenly widened his eyes. He said, "You know, Stoneship Woods scares every kid in Carrolton completely dry of spit."

"Right," said Cyril.

"So maybe we should explore."

Cyril looked uneasy. "I don't follow your logic there, Magellan."

"Well, it's just like a device—say, a halogen lamp," said Lucas.

"Stoneship is?"

"Right!" said Lucas, now bouncing with energy. "How does it work? It's a mystery, and so my mom is scared to death of it. She's pretty sure our halogen lamp will explode in flames at any moment, so she wants to toss it in the Carrolton landfill."

Cyril looked clearly confused.

"But if you get *inside* the device—take it apart and take a look—the mystery goes away," said Lucas. "We could do that to Stoneship Woods!"

"Did you take apart your halogen lamp?" asked Lexi.

"Yes."

"What happened?"

"It exploded in flames."

All three stared into the dusky forest. There was a long

pause during which loud, scary music played—no, wait, this is a book, not a movie. Okay, the scary music played inside each kid's head—yes, as if each wore headphones that played the soundtrack of a horror movie in which slobbering, demented beasts rip the guts out of stupid teenagers. Okay, maybe that's too much. Let's just say the kids were tense.

Suddenly something clapped its paw on Cyril's shoulder. The three kids jumped and shrieked. But it was just Jake.

"Hey, the game's over," said Jake. "No need to scream. Not anymore, anyway."

The others looked ill.

"We lost, big-time," said Jake happily. "But I'm only hemorrhaging a little bit, so let's go to Dairy Queen and celebrate."

Nobody spoke. Jake followed their gaze.

"What are we looking at, guys?" asked Jake.

Deep in Stoneship Woods, bushes shuddered in the breeze—not unlike grim, monstrous forces deployed to devour a foolish expedition.

THE SECRET OF
STONESHIP WOODS

The four Bixbys plus Cyril and Lexi rode the trolley back to the Soccer Complex entrance. There, the Bixby parents kissed their sons good-bye and strolled off holding hands—a sight Jake Bixby always found immensely reassuring.

"We'll meet you at McDonald's for some ice cream cones!" called Mrs. Bixby.

"Okay, Mom."

"Half an hour," called Mr. Bixby. "I'm buying!"

Mr. and Mrs. Bixby laughed heartily at this parent joke. Jake liked it when his dad made jokes, even if they were extremely lame, like, most of the time. The brothers waved after their parents for a while, then looked at each other.

Jake said, "Ready, bud?"

"Let's do it, man," said Lucas.

Lucas turned to Lexi, who smiled. They slapped right hands while pointing at each other with their left hand. They'd seen NBA players do this, except in a much taller way.

Jake nodded at Cyril, who now looked green around the gills.

"Mad adventure skills," said Jake. "You ready, dude?"

Cyril said, "No."

"Why not?"

"I'm convinced this is a mistake."

Jake nodded. "You're probably right," he said.

The four friends trooped out the main gate. Then they turned and followed the high fence around the east edge of the Soccer Complex.

Trees are friendly, as a rule.

But when kids are scared, even happy trees suddenly become creepy and depraved. It's a phenomenon that dates back to the early days of ancient Mesopotamia. Branches transform into spiky, twisted arms that try to grab you, and so on and so forth. Why this happens, nobody knows. It just does. Scientists have tried to explain it, but further studies are needed.

Unfortunately for the four explorers, Stoneship Woods was worse than most.

Overhanging limbs, gnarled and crisscrossing, nearly

blocked out all sunlight. Wind gusts moaned through the leaves. To make matters worse, a light rain began to fall just as Jake, Lucas, Cyril, and Lexi approached the first scraggly trees. Try to imagine a dark, dripping, moaning, gloomy forest with a really bad reputation. Dark things loom left and right, just out of sight. *What's that? What's moving?*

Cyril pushed under a low-hanging branch. Suddenly a swarm of black fluttery things fell onto him. He started screaming.

"Spiders!" he screamed.

He thrashed around, taking wild swipes at his head. "They're attacking! They're eating my hair!" He fell to the ground and started rolling around. "My gosh, they're cold! They're slimy!"

The other three watched him for a while. Then Lexi said, "Hold still."

She reached down and brushed a clump of wet leaves off Cyril's neck.

"Are they off?" yelled Cyril.

"Yes," said Lexi.

"All of them?"

Lexi looked down at Cyril for a few moments. Then she said, "You're clear, man."

Jake tried his famous grin, but could manage only a small upward lip twitch on one side. He was calm, as usual, but unsure of his bearings. Up ahead, tree trunks of all sizes grew so close together it looked like The Picket Fence of Insanity. In the grim darkness Jake couldn't see any way through.

"Where was that concrete wall you saw?" he asked.

Lucas said, "Under a big tree. Wasn't it, guys?"

"Yeah."

"Where?"

"Aha!" Lucas pointed toward a huge cottonwood tree that loomed above the tree line like a hideous sentinel of doom. "Over there."

"Yeah," agreed Lexi. "That's it."

She rushed ahead, hopping lightly as a wood sprite over fallen limbs. Her long dark tresses bobbed as she leaped to a low branch and swung through a high, narrow opening in the fence of trees. Behind her, Lucas gazed in astonishment as his best buddy disappeared gracefully into the gloom.

"That kid is amazing," said Cyril, who was finally on his feet again.

"Amen to that," said Jake.

"Her mom makes her audition for *The Nutcracker*, like, *every* Christmas," said Lucas.

Cyril said, "Well, all those years of being a dancing petunia have clearly paid off."

They listened to Lexi rustling leaves. Then, suddenly, there was silence.

"Lexi?" called Jake.

Silence.

"Yo, Lexi, dude!" yelled Lucas. "You there, man?"

A loud *crack* sounded to their left, just down the tree line.

"Oh, no!" said Cyril, looking sick.

"What?" asked Lucas. "What?"

"I know that sound."

"What is it?"

Cyril turned to him. He took a deep breath and whispered: *"Bone marrow!"*

"What are you talking about?" asked Lucas.

"There's only one way to extract it." Cyril twisted his hands as if snapping a bone in half. Lucas watched, horrified. Then Cyril hissed, "Bears consider human bone marrow a delicacy."

They heard another series of cracks. Lucas looked nauseous. Suddenly a small birch crashed to the ground, opening a narrow hole in the line of trees. Lexi's head popped through.

"Rotted trunk," she said.

"Good job, Lexi!" said Jake.

The three boys scrambled through the hole. On the other side of the tree line rose a tall security fence with spirals of barbed wire strung across the top. Behind that, a white concrete wall rose even higher. Jake stared at the windowless, bunkerlike building. A thick metal door looked sealed shut.

Above the door, sandblasted into the concrete, was the name:

STONESHIP TOYS
Midwest Warehouse

Jaws dropped open as the four kids stared. Slowly a new feeling spread across the team.

"A *toy* factory?" said Lucas.

"Better," said Cyril. "A toy *warehouse*. You know, where they store stuff."

"You think there's, like, *toys* in there?"

"Maybe."

"How many?"

"Like, a zillion, maybe."

Cyril and Lucas immediately boosted Lexi up the fence, but the barbed wire at the top stymied her progress. Meanwhile Jake walked along the perimeter. Wild overgrowth everywhere suggested the place had been abandoned long ago. As he approached the corner, Jake could see the main gate. It was wide open!

He looked back at the others.

Lexi, clinging to the fence with one hand, was trying to saw through a vicious coil of barbed wire with a finger-nail file. Below her, the other two barked encouragement.

"How much longer?" shouted Lucas with excitement.

"Couple months," said Lexi.

"Guys, check this out," called Jake.

Lexi dropped and Jake led the team into an industrial-looking entrance yard. An asphalt driveway, badly cracked and overgrown with weeds, disappeared into the woods in one direction. It curved through the gate and around behind the warehouse. The foursome followed the driveway to a loading dock on the building's far side.

Three massive cargo doors lined the wall behind the dock. All were shut, except one. It was raised just a few inches. It looked extremely heavy, almost like a blast door, and a few group tugs confirmed this fact. Before anyone could speak, Lexi was shimmying feetfirst under the door.

Just before her head disappeared into the warehouse, she stopped. She looked at Jake and said, "You don't suppose there's any, you know . . . ?"

"Bad guys?"

"No, that's not what I was thinking."

"Beasts? Bad things?"

"No."

"Lexi," said Cyril, "you have to learn to articulate your feelings." He shook his head. "Women are so poor at that."

"Any, uh, like, you know," said Lexi, turning her hand back and forth.

"Baseballs?"

"No," said Lexi. "Like, door switches."

Jake looked over at Lucas, who was fiddling with a

small hatch on the wall. He flipped something. The massive door groaned and slid upward.

"Dang!" said Lucas. He walked over to Lexi. "Geez, I'm glad I didn't, like, crush you."

The kids crept inside.

The main floor of the warehouse was deserted except for stacks of wooden shipping pallets and a few empty cartons labeled STONESHIP TOY COMPANY. A loading crane on a metal track hung from the ceiling. High in one corner, a room with big windows jutted out over the warehouse floor. But the friends could find no way to reach this room—no ladder, stairs, or ramp.

"I bet that's the control room," said Lucas, gazing up at the windows.

Jake knew what his brother was thinking.

"Yes," he said. "Imagine all the factory control gizmos up there. The switches and levers and stuff. The technology must be amazing."

Jake smiled, knowing that if there was a way to reach the control room, Lucas would find it. He wandered over to Cyril, who was reading a packing slip he'd found on the floor.

"Jake, you ever heard of Stoneship Toys?" asked Cyril.

"Nope," said Jake.

"I know every toy company that ever existed," said Cyril. "Back when I was a little kid, couple years ago, I used to keep a database. Remember?"

"Oh, yeah," nodded Jake. "Wasn't that your second-grade science project?"

"Yes, and I've never heard of Stoneship Toys." Cyril held up the packing slip. "Man, according to this, they packed a shipment of two thousand 'Space Shuttle Console Simulators' bound for Schenectady, New York. I'm telling you, Jake," said Cyril with intensity, "I would have known about this!"

A loud mechanical whine made them both jump.

"What's that?"

"I don't know."

Above them, the loading crane began to slide down its ceiling track. As it moved, its huge, three-pronged claw slowly opened. Cyril screamed.

"It's alive!"

Lexi ran up to them, staring at the claw. "Where's Lucas?" she asked.

Jake turned to look.

Lucas was gone!

The crane stopped directly above them.

The claw opened and closed a few times, making a loud chomping sound. Then it began to lower.

The kids backed away.

When the claw reached ground level, it pivoted. Slowly and deliberately, it raised one of its fingerlike prongs. The prong seemed to be pointing at the raised control room. Jake frowned, looking up at the window. Then he grinned.

Lucas waved down at them.

"Dude!" said Lexi, waving back.

"How'd he get up there?" asked Cyril, looking around.

Jake approached the wall directly beneath the control room. He heard a whirring noise. In the wall a series of ascending slots opened one by one revealing recessed rungs. A ladder! At the top, a hatch slid open on the underside of the control room. Jake climbed quickly, followed by Cyril and Lexi.

In the room, Lucas sat waiting in a plush leather chair, hands behind his head.

"This place intensely rocks," he said.

"Holy monkey!" said Cyril, looking around.

Behind Lucas was a large console filled with monitors, keyboards, dials, levers, lights, and displays of every kind imaginable. Along the back wall, a low shelf held a variety of cool-looking gadgets and devices.

"This is better than toys," said Lexi, eyes popping.

Jake looked around in awe.

"*Way* better," he said.

⑤

GADGETS AND GIZMOS

Yes, the Stoneship control room was amazing—gadgets and gizmos galore—far cooler than an entire warehouse of toys, even. But what exactly *was* all this stuff? Where did it come from? What was it used for?

And who left it here?

"I have theories," said Cyril. He was tapping commands into one of the console keyboards.

"I'll bet you do," said Jake, trying to watch over Cyril's shoulder. This was not easy because of Cyril's hair.

Cyril scanned the bank of monitors. Odd data scrolled down the screens. He tapped another key and the data flow stopped. "Interesting," he said. "I just wish I knew what I was doing."

"Technical knowledge is overrated," said Jake. "Just push buttons until something happens."

Cyril nodded. "Okay," he said.

Jake said, "So, come on, tell me your theories."

"Well, to begin with, I really don't think Stoneship was a legitimate toy company," said Cyril, glancing up at Jake.

"Why not?" asked Jake.

"Because other than that obviously bogus packing slip downstairs, I have yet to find a single piece of data that has anything to do with toys," said Cyril. "No orders or invoices. No inventory lists. Nothing that suggests the manufacture and shipping of toys—well, other than *this*."

Cyril turned back to the keyboard and monitors and tapped in a Web site address: www.stoneshiptoys.com. Jake pushed a chunk of Cyril's hair aside to watch. On-screen, a home page appeared asking for a code entry.

"What kind of toy company would demand a *secret code* for access to its Web site?" asked Cyril indignantly.

"Seems odd," admitted Jake.

Cyril turned to give Jake a significant look. "Dude, I think this Web site, just like this whole warehouse, is a front operation."

"A front for what?"

"I don't know. I haven't found any unlocking data yet."

"Well, what *have* you found?" asked Jake.

"This." Cyril clicked on an icon. "This image is the only interesting file I can open so far."

A bright, colorful map opened on the screen. It looked

like one of those swirling weather maps you see on *The Nightly News at Nine.*

"I'm pretty sure this is a satellite shot of Carrolton," said Cyril. He pointed at a big green patch on the map. "See? That's the Soccer Complex."

"You can see it from outer space?" asked Jake, leaning in to look more closely.

"I'm sure you can see it from Jupiter."

"Aha," said Jake. "I see. So there's Stoneship Woods, then."

"Right."

"And that must be our warehouse," said Jake, pointing to a tiny white square. Then something struck him. "Say, is this a live satellite shot? Looking down, like, right now?"

Cyril clicked on the screen. The image zoomed in closer. Both boys watched intently. Cyril clicked again for even more magnification.

"Yeah, look at the cars in that parking lot," said Cyril. "See?"

"They're moving," said Jake.

Cyril clicked again to zoom in even further. Then he dragged the view directly over the Stoneship warehouse. He zoomed in one more time. The picture was a little fuzzy by now, but you could definitely make out the warehouse loading dock.

Jake immediately headed for the ladder, scrambled

down to the warehouse floor, and jogged out through the cargo doors onto the loading dock. He looked straight up into the sky and waved.

When he returned to the control room, Cyril looked pale.

"Did you see me?" asked Jake.

Cyril said, "Yes."

Jake punched the air. "That's *so* cool!"

But Cyril didn't share Jake's enthusiasm. Mutely he just stared at the screen.

"What's wrong?" said Jake.

"Why would a toy company need its own surveillance satellite?" asked Cyril weakly.

Jake thought, then nodded. "Now *that's* a pretty good question," he said.

"Satellites cost, like, a gazillion bucks," said Cyril. "It would take a pretty powerful company—or *agency*—to have one."

"Maybe Stoneship Toys just uses it, or shares it with other companies."

"But that doesn't answer the question *Why do they need it?* And anyway, sharing it, that's another disturbing thought," said Cyril, eyes widening. "Maybe somebody else is getting this satellite feed."

Jake looked at Cyril, feeling a chill. His friend's paranoia was starting to infect him, too.

"Jake, if I can see you on the loading dock," said Cyril,

motioning at the monitor, "then maybe somebody else can too."

"You mean"—Jake was thinking hard—"maybe somebody knows we're here. Right now."

"That's precisely what I mean."

Meanwhile, Lucas and Lexi examined the various devices in the room.

"A lot of this stuff is pretty easy to figure out," said Lucas, setting a small metal case on the counter. "This, for example, is an electronic Spy Tracker System."

"Wow," said Lexi. "How can you tell?"

Lucas held the case closer to Lexi's face. The words "Spy Tracker System" were engraved in the metal.

"Aha," said Lexi.

"Check it out, man," said Lucas. He slid back a latch and opened the case, revealing three ball-like gadgets and a green display screen with an eight-by-eight grid. "You place these sensor pods around the area you want to monitor, then sketch the area dimensions and pod locations on this grid. When movement activates a sensor, it flashes on the grid. See?"

Lexi looked at the open screen for a few seconds. Then she looked up at Lucas and said, "I have no idea what you're talking about."

Lucas moved along the shelf from gadget to gadget, touching each one respectfully—okay, maybe a better word would be "lovingly." Lucas truly *loved* gadgets. He adored gizmos. He worshipped widgets and whatsits. For him, finding this room was like hitting the Bridal Chamber motherlode in New Mexico and seeing walls of pure silver ore.

"Lexi!" he said. "These are hands-free Spy Link walkie-talkies."

Eight headsets hung on a small rack. Lucas grabbed one, slipped its earphone over his ear, and clipped the receiver on his belt. A small, slim mouthpiece curved down from the earphone to his mouth. Lexi took another set from the rack and hooked herself up. Both kids flicked small activation buttons on the receiver.

"Can you hear me, Lexi?"

"Yes."

"This is fabulous! This is amazing!"

"Okay."

"I can't believe this! Can you?"

"Not entirely, no."

Lucas continued down the line of gadgets. He slipped a heavy-duty set of Spy Vision Goggles onto his forehead and lowered them over his eyes. Night vision! Next was a handheld electronic listening device called a Spy Supersonic Ear. Then came a peculiar pair of sunglasses with a lens-mounted camera, followed by an amazing Spy Pen with multiple functions. Plus lots of other special scopes and goggles and tool kits.

The last device on the shelf stumped Lucas, however.

It was a small silver case with a recessed video screen that looked kind of like an Etch A Sketch. But the casing was perfectly smooth! No knobs to turn, no buttons or keys to press. No screws or seams or indentations of any kind. The only features were a small symbol embossed in a corner and a single word flashing on the screen: "OMEGA."

"What is this thing?" asked Lucas.

"You don't know?" asked Lexi, slightly stunned.

"No."

"Wow." Lexi looked at the device with wary respect. She touched the screen. "What does Omega mean?"

"It's the last letter of the Greek alphabet," said Lucas. He pointed at the embossed symbol: Ω. "That's it, I think."

"It comes last?"

"Right."

Lexi nodded.

Lucas shook the Omega Link. It felt solid, and nothing rattled inside. He shrugged, put it down, and said, "It must be a surveillance mechanism, or maybe a mobile communications link, or something." He shrugged again. "Like, whatever."

Jake and Cyril pondered whether to stay and keep messing around with stuff, or to run away before the guys in black suits and sunglasses arrived and hauled them off to Guantanamo, Cuba.

But being thirteen years old, the boys found the choice easy to make.

"After all, nothing bad ever happens in Carrolton," said Cyril.

"True."

"Even when my parents yell at each other, they always explain that it's not my fault," said Cyril.

Jake patted his buddy's back. Cyril's parents were notorious fighters. Suddenly Jake remembered: "Parents! Oh my golly! We're supposed to be at McDonald's!" He checked his watch. "Oh, no!"

Cyril whipped a cell phone out of his back pocket. He said, "Telecom?"

"Thanks, dude."

Jake dialed his mom's cell phone. He was used to telling the truth, so this would be tricky. After an initial apology, Jake canceled the McDonald's date with his folks.

"Oh, that's okay," said Mrs. Bixby. "Don't worry about us. You'll be gone soon, on your own. I guess your father and I had better get used to it."

"Mom, I'm only thirteen years old."

"Time flies," she said. "Sunrise, sunset."

"Okay, well . . . I won't be gone for, like, five years at the soonest."

"Don't feel guilty, honey."

"I'm not!"

"Your father and I really have a lot of work to do this weekend anyway, a tremendous amount, actually, but we haven't been sitting here too long, just eating ice cream, waiting. Only forty-five minutes or so."

"I'm really sorry, Mom."

"Don't feel guilty, honey."

"Yeah, you said that."

"Okay, honey. Well, I guess we'll just head on home now and get in some productive time finally."

"Okay, see you soon."

"Bye. Hope you're having fun at least, if you're not doing anything productive."

"I am."

"Bye, honey!"

"Bye, Mom."

"See you at home, hopefully soon."

"Okay."

"Miss you."

Jake rolled his eyes. "Miss you too."

Cyril, trying to suppress laughter, let out an enormously loud snort.

"Honey, what was that?" asked Mrs. Bixby.

"What?"

"That odd, piglike sound."

"Oh, well, that was Cyril. He, like, sneezed."

"You're with Cyril?"

"Yes, I am."

Cyril started rolling on the ground, laughing. He had to hold his stomach so his guts wouldn't spill out all over the floor tiles.

"Oh, Okay. Well, then, see you later."

"Bye, Mom."

"Love you!"

"Love you too." Jake quickly pushed the End Call button. "*Great flying monkeys!*" he yelled.

Lucas walked over. "Was that Mom?" he asked.

"Yes! Yes, it was Mom."

"It most certainly was," howled Cyril, tears in his eyes.

"Did she want to talk to me?" said Lucas, reaching for the phone.

"*No!*" yelled Jake and Cyril in unison.

A while later all four kids stood around the main monitor, chattering advice to Cyril, who clacked away at the keyboard. Being modern kids, they all had some experience at hacking past firewalls and passwords. But nothing was working.

"This stuff is seriously encrypted," said Cyril.

"You mean, like, super secret code?" asked Lexi.

"Something like that," said Cyril, typing. "High level stuff. Very sophisticated. I can't figure out where to get started or what to run here."

For the past hour Cyril had been trying to tap into the Stoneship computer system. The long console desk ran under the main window overlooking the warehouse floor. One big video monitor was right in the middle. Four smaller screens, two on each side of the main monitor, were filled with nothing but fuzzy static.

"Type 'Open Sesame,'" said Lucas, who was jumping up and down like an insane baboon.

"Hey, check this out," said Cyril.

He clicked on a file icon. On the screen, the following appeared:

T3 Surveillance Protocol
Priority: RED
Status: ONGOING
Code: _____

"Surveillance protocol?" said Cyril.

"Hmmm," said Jake. "Looks like maybe somebody was spying on somebody else."

"Apparently you type in a code here," said Cyril.

"What kind of code?"

Cyril looked at him. "A secret code," he said.

"What kind of secret code?"

"Well, if I knew, it wouldn't be *secret*, now, would it?"

Jake looked over at the shelf where all the gadgetry sat in rows. A sudden chill went up his spine. What was the secret behind this odd place? He went to the window overlooking the warehouse floor. Empty, forlorn—not a hint of previous occupants. Where did they go? Were they still alive? As Jake backed away from the glass, the glare of the control room lights drifted like ghosts across the pane.

"How many characters in the code?" asked Lucas.

Cyril moved the cursor under the code blank. "Five," he said.

"Five?" said Lucas.

"Yes, five."

"Five," said Jake, thinking.

Cyril said, "Five, correct. It's that funny one that comes *right after four,* I believe."

"Five?" asked Lexi suddenly.

Cyril looked at Lexi. "Have I lost my mind?" he asked.

"Try 'Omega,'" said Lexi.

"Why?"

Lucas brightened. "Hey, yeah," he said. "Omega!"

Cyril looked at Jake, who shrugged. Then Cyril said, "Why?"

Lucas hurried over and grabbed the Omega Link from the gadget shelf. He showed it to the older boys. "I can't figure out what this thing does," he said. "But maybe the word means something."

"It has five letters," nodded Jake.

"All right," said Cyril. And he typed it in.

The main monitor suddenly flashed this phrase: "OMEGA LINK."

The four subsidiary screens flickered to life too. All four beeped and displayed different camera views of a familiar-looking structure. The four friends stared in awe, then looked at one another.

"That's the Old Farmhouse," said Jake.

"The haunted one?" asked Cyril.

"Yeah," said Jake. "The haunted one."

Rumors about the old place out on Route 36 were as rich as the ones about Stoneship Woods. Kids claimed to have seen The Old Farmer himself, wandering his overgrown, untended wheat field. He was said to wear a hockey mask and carry a Bolivian machete, or maybe an axe, although others said his superhumanly powerful bloody hands were the only weapons he needed.

"So this is an observation post," said Cyril.

"Apparently so," said Jake.

"A spy post."

"And this is all spy gear," said Lucas. "No wonder it's so cool!"

Everyone stared at the surveillance screens. As the kids watched, the sky slowly darkened. Then, inside the farmhouse, red lights flickered on, illuminating the windows.

The Farmer was awake.

(6)

THE OLD FARMHOUSE

Dark, chilling legends of "The Farmer" had drifted around Carrolton for years.

The Old Farmhouse hunkered in the middle of forty ragged acres on the town's southwest corner. Over the years, Carrolton suburbs had slowly crept around the weed-infested farm. Now it was very valuable property. Real estate guys wanted to buy it, rezone it, and build a shopping "theme village"—basically, a bunch of fake stuff that looks real, plus four hundred movie theaters.

But The Farmer wouldn't sell out. And soon the questions began:

Why did he turn down millions for his land?

Who is he?

What evil secret is he hiding?

What's the capital of Kenya? Can you name its major exports?

These sorts of questions haunted the children of Carrolton. Imaginations ran wild. Cyril, for example, believed The Farmer was interbreeding turkeys and bacteria to create a mutant strain that would infect everybody with the urge to gobble. Reasonable kids like Jake Bixby could easily discount such speculation as wild fantasy. Now, however, Jake stared at four good reasons why the Old Farmhouse was indeed an eerie, mysterious place.

"Four camera angles," said Cyril. "Wow!"

"Looks like the cameras were placed to observe all four sides of the house," noted Jake.

"Right," nodded Cyril. "They didn't want anyone coming or going without being seen. Clearly they wish to document his grisly, murderous activities."

"What a setup."

"Yeah, big-time spy stuff."

"Can you zoom in?" asked Jake.

Cyril clicked on a small icon shaped like a telescope in the corner of one screen. Sure enough, the view zoomed closer to the farmhouse. As with the satellite shot on the main monitor, Cyril could click and drag the camera view wherever he wanted. But several minutes of zooming and panning revealed nothing new or interesting about the Old Farmhouse.

"All of the shades are drawn tight," said Jake.

"Yeah, you can't see a thing," said Cyril.

"Maybe that's why the spies abandoned this warehouse," suggested Lucas. "They gave up."

"Sure," said Cyril. "And when my dad can't find a parking spot at the mall, he just stops on the road, gets out, *and abandons the car.*"

Lexi said, "He does?"

"Yes," said Cyril. "We have to buy a new car almost every time dad goes shopping."

"That's nuts!" said Lexi.

Cyril gaped in disbelief at Lexi for a second. Then he shook his head and stood up. "Little kids are so gullible," he said.

Jake faced his buddy. "So you're saying we don't have a satisfactory explanation for this place yet."

"Right!" Cyril pounded a fist into his hand. "Look around, will you, guys? See this? And this?" Cyril indicated thick cobwebs, and the disgusting, half-full coffee cups on the console. "This place was abandoned pretty quickly, many months ago. Why would somebody just *walk out* on, like, eight bajillion dollars worth of high-tech equipment?"

Nobody had an answer.

Cyril said, "Okay, now think about *this*. Our amazing observation post was set up"—he pointed at the house on the screen—"to observe that vile, malignant nest of agricultural depravity. Now, suppose The Farmer found out he was being observed? Suppose he traced the surveillance *back to this warehouse!*"

"How would he do that?" asked Jake.

"I don't know. Smell, maybe."

"Smell?"

"Whatever," said Cyril. "Somehow he tracks the spies back to their spy den." He looked around with big eyes, nodding. "I think you see where this is going."

"You're saying he wiped them out?"

"Exactly."

Lucas looked around. "But I see no signs of struggle," he said. "No blood, nothing ransacked, nothing out of place. Looks to me like people just walked out . . . and never came back."

Cyril slid his eyes sideways, thinking. "Okay, so maybe he lured them out. To his farm! All of them!"

"How?"

"I don't know," said Cyril, irritated. "Why are you asking me all these questions?"

Jake sat on the edge of the console, staring at the Old Farmhouse on one of the monitors. The sun had set behind it. Against the backdrop of the pink western sky, the black house looked menacing and alive. Then Jake turned to the others.

"Let's think logically here," he said.

Lucas smiled. Whenever his big brother said that, focus always followed.

"Whoever abandoned Stoneship was very interested in activities at the Old Farmhouse," said Jake, nodding at the monitors. "That's the only given we have. Now, I know that life isn't always black and white, but let's assume one side is the Good Guys and one side is the Evildoers." He glanced at Cyril and said, "Which side is which, do you think?"

Cyril looked at the decrepit, scary old house on the screen.

"That seems obvious," he said.

"Is it?" Jake turned to the two younger kids. He said, "What do *you* think?"

Lexi said, "Me?"

"Yeah, you."

Lexi looked at Lucas. "Is this a trick?" she asked.

"No," said Lucas, grinning. "Jake believes that everybody's input is important. I have no idea where he got such a misguided notion."

Lexi walked over to the shelf of gadgets. She picked up a pair of Spy Vision Goggles. Then she pulled them down her forehead and snapped them over her eyes. "Do bad guys need cool spy stuff like this?"

"It's possible," said Lucas, watching his buddy.

"But not probable," said Lexi.

"Why not?" asked Jake, watching Lexi carefully.

"Bad guys just *do* bad stuff," said Lexi. "So the good guys have to *watch* them."

Lucas caught the drift. He said, "Yeah, good guys wait patiently until bad guys do something bad."

"Wait and watch."

"Exactly."

"So they can catch them in the act and arrest them, like, legally."

Jake nodded. "Okay," he said. "That makes sense."

Some instinct told Jake Stoneship was legitimate—a law enforcement operation, maybe. The technology here suggested high-level involvement—maybe a government agency like the FBI. But he saw no evidence yet of what "evil" these high-tech cops were looking for in the Old Farmhouse. Counterfeiting? Drugs? Fringe hate groups? Or perhaps the dreaded *T* word— terrorist activity?

Suddenly something caught Cyril's eye.

He spun to one of the monitors and pointed. He whispered, *"Look!"*

The foursome froze.

A black silhouette moved slowly across the red glow of a farmhouse window shade. The shape was huge. You could make out a massive head, a body, and huge arms. Everyone stared, transfixed. All of a sudden the arms started flailing, like a wild carnivore shredding meat from the bones of its kill, or maybe just waving happily to a really cute little child, depending on your point of view. (Three guesses how the kids saw it.) After a few seconds, the freakish evil shadow disappeared. The frozen kids continued to stare at the screen.

"Okay," said Jake.

Everybody turned to him.

He said, "*That* was scary."

Lucas slumped to the floor. Jake looked around the room.

"Decision time," he said.

He turned to Cyril first.

"What?" said Cyril.

"So what do we do here?" asked Jake.

"Okay, I vote we go home and make hot cocoa and watch, like, a Christmas movie with Bing Crosby and stuff," said Cyril.

"In September?"

"Yes, in September."

Lucas, lying on his back, raised his hand slowly.

"Yes?" said Jake.

Lucas stood up. "Given our present capabilities, Jake," he said in his deepest voice. But he stopped. He started again, voice slowly rising, "I think, you know, like, given the tools at our disposal, that we can essentially, more or less, uh, the moral imperative seems, well, you know, I'm, uh, I'm going to sit down now." He sat back down.

Jake turned to Lexi.

Lexi was still wearing the goggles. She looked like a mutant insect that, for some reason, decided to pull on a soccer uniform when it woke up in the hive. She picked up a small gadget.

"This is a remote listening device," said Lexi. "A bug."

"I know," said Jake.

"It's very sensitive."

"Right."

"When planted, it lets you hear everything."

"I believe that's correct."

Lexi looked up at Jake. "Where do you want me to plant it?" she said.

Jake nodded, grinning big. He pointed at the farmhouse on the nearest monitor screen.

"How about there?" he said.

Even in happy Carrolton, parents are uneasy about letting their children roam unattended at night. So Jake had to do some fast talking.

"Orthotics?" asked his mom.

Jake held the cell phone a couple of feet away from his ear. His mother's phone voice could pierce steel. He said, "Yeah, you know—those things you stick in your shoes?"

"I *know* what orthotics are. Why would Cyril leave them at the soccer field?"

"Good question." Jake looked over at Cyril, who grabbed his foot and mouthed the words "Blister! Blister!" "He had a blister."

"I don't like you out there at night."

"The grounds crew is there. Watering. Dozens of guys, maybe hundreds."

"The fields have automatic sprinklers, honey."

"Exactly. And if they go off, Cyril's orthotics will, like, disintegrate?"

"Orthotics are plastic."

"Plastic?" Jake watched Cyril pantomime something. "Uh, no. They aren't. They are . . . something else. Something chopping? Something . . . something that is . . . wood? They're wood! Right, and you know, Mom, if wooden orthotics get wet, they warp and, and then, like, slivers just like go *boiiing!* and stick out, and Cyril, well, he—"

"He cries like a wounded marmoset!" hissed Cyril.

"He cries like a wounded marmoset," said Jake with a grimace.

There was a long silence on the other end of the phone. Then, finally: "Hurry."

"We'll hurry, Mom."

"Good-bye." Click.

Jake stared at Cyril. "She hung up."

"No," said Cyril. "She must have been cut off by a bad connection. A solar storm, maybe."

"No, she said good-bye and hung up."

Cyril was stunned. "Your mom *never* just hangs up."

"I know."

"Well," said Cyril, "I find *that* disturbing."

The two younger kids, Lucas and Lexi, trooped along behind as they wound around yet another Carrolton cul-de-sac. Lucas had a canvas backpack slung over his shoulder. He pulled it open and distributed walkie-talkie headsets to everyone.

"Time to mount up, guys," he said.

Then he handed the tiny microphone bug to Lexi.

The Ridgeview Estates subdevelopment bordered the dark, fallow acreage of the Old Farmhouse. Homes in Ridgeview Estates were not really estates, nor could one view a ridge within five hundred miles in any direction. But they were nice houses, anyway.

The four hiked down a winding trail through a playground to an ominous-looking fence that separated the neighborhood from the farm property. Jake started to climb through the split rails.

"Wait a minute!" said Lucas suddenly.

"What?" said Cyril, spinning around. "Who's there? Who's tailing us?"

Lexi patted Cyril's arm. "Nobody."

"Then what is it?" yelled Cyril. *"Who's after us?"*

"Well, I was just thinking," said Lucas. "Before we go in-country, shouldn't we come up with a name?"

Cyril said, "A name for what?"

"For us."

"You mean, like, 'The Super Spy Guys' or something?"

said Cyril, wiping cold sweat from his brow.

Jake looked over at his brother and said, "Yeah, what do you have in mind?"

Lucas hefted his backpack. "This spy gear is the most amazing stuff I've ever seen, more amazing than even I could have possibly imagined. With the kind of technical capability provided by this, you know, this *spy* gear, I foresee some wicked tight reconnaissance work . . ."

"Hmm," said Jake. "So you mean something like, uh, 'Spy Gear,' I don't know . . . 'Team . . . Reconnaissance . . . Unit'?"

"Yeah, but shorten it to . . . 'Spy Gear Ghost Team Recon'!" said Lucas.

"That sounds stupid," said Lexi.

The Bixbys both looked at her.

"Excellent point," said Jake, patting Lexi's shoulder.

"I like being called Lexi," said Lexi.

Lucas said, "Well, yeah. I guess we don't need some cheesy name." But he looked disappointed, and folded his arms. "It's not like we're the X-Men or whatever."

Jake said, "How about we just call ourselves 'the Spy Gear team'?" He glanced at Lexi.

Lexi looked over at Lucas.

Then Jake said, "Or maybe, like . . . 'Team Spy Gear'?"

Lucas brightened. "That works." He nodded. "Says it all, really."

Lexi said, "Sure."

Jake turned to Cyril and said, "Cyril? Your input?"

Cyril was staring over the jagged line of weeds at the Old Farmhouse. Beyond the fence, dark stalks waved in the breeze. To Cyril, they looked like spears of some brutal goblin army. A pale moon shimmered in the sky. Off in the distance, you could hear a barn owl hoot.

Cyril put his hand on the fence. To him it seemed the boundary between civilization and chaos.

"Team Spy Gear," he said.

"Yeah! So what do you think?"

Cyril said, "I think I'd rather not."

TEAM SPY GEAR:
CASE NO. 0001

And so Team Spy Gear fanned out around the Old Farmhouse, according to plan.

As in all good horror movies, the team split up and headed to four separate positions.

That way, the Monster could pick them off one by one.

Go Team One

Jake knelt in a dense thicket about fifty yards behind the house. From here, he had a good view. Moon-cast shadows infested the clearing. Every clump of weeds seemed to spread dark tentacles across the ground, ready to grab kids.

Jake eyed the big willow tree that hung over the south porch of the Old Farmhouse.

"Check, check," he said quietly. His voice-activated, hands-free Spy Link headset let him talk while pushing weeds aside for a better look. "All units report. Where are you, Go Team?"

Cyril's voice echoed in Jake's ear: **Roger, Go Team Three copies loud and clear, over.** He sounded like an astronaut reporting to Mission Control, except of course he could never get a space helmet over his hair.

Go Team Two here! That was Lucas. He sounded a little scared, but excited.

I'm here, mumbled another voice.

There was a pause. Then Jake asked, "Is that you, Go Team Four?"

It's Lexi, said Lexi.

"Roger."

No, Lexi.

"Whatever. Are you in position? Can you see the house yet?"

Yes.

Cyril spoke in a voice made husky by raw fear. **Go Team One, have you deployed to your designated observation coordinates, over?**

Nervous as he was, Jake found this amusing. He listened to Cyril's heavy, serious breathing. "Yes, I'm here. What about you?"

Negative, negative, came the raspy answer. **There's something stretched across the ground here, like a vine or . . . I don't know. I'm backing away in case it's some kind of *aaaaaaah!***

Jake heard a thud. "Cyril?"

I'm okay. I just—wait, what is this stuff?

"Cyril?"

No answer.

"Are you okay, Go Team Three?"

Of course I'm—*aaahh*! Jake could hear something crack. Then, after a few seconds of gasping and moaning, Cyril's voice piped up again. He said, Well, now that was interesting.

"What's going on?"

Don't ask. More rustling sounds. Okay, okay, I'm in position now.

Jake raised a slick-looking pair of binoculars to his eyes. Night was transformed into emerald day through the Spy Night Scope, and Jake swept his enhanced view across the clearing. After a few seconds, he said, "Go Team Two, I don't see you yet."

I'm going in now, whispered Lucas.

Jake trained the scope on a scrub pine wiggling at the left edge of the clearing.

"Ah," he said. "Got you marked."

Go Team Two

Lucas set aside the fake scrub pine he'd fashioned from loose branches. He waved in Jake's direction, then shrugged off his gadget backpack and pulled out the gray Spy Tracker case.

He said, "Okay, Phase Alpha is go."

Excellent, replied Jake. Go Team, full alert. All eyes on Phase Alpha deployment.

I've got my scope on him, said Cyril.

I see him too, said Lexi.

Lucas opened the case and removed three ball-shaped sensor pods. They were labeled SENSOR I, SENSOR II, and SENSOR III. He unsnapped a side pocket of his cargo pants and dropped in all three sensors.

"Okay, I'll be observing radio silence for the next ten minutes," he said, adjusting his Spy Link headset. "Uh, unless of course I get attacked."

Of course, said Cyril. If the Monster attacks and, like, burrows into your thorax to implant alien spawn, scream really loud.

"Very funny."

I'm entirely serious. It'll give the rest of us time to escape.

Don't worry, bro," Lucas heard Jake say. We got your back.

Phase Alpha was simple.

The goal: Place Spy Tracker sensor pods in a triangle around the Old Farmhouse.

This way Team Spy Gear could monitor The Farmer's insidious moves. Whenever a pod detected significant movement, the Spy Tracker base station—consisting of a map, a speaker, and three light emitting diode (LED) trip lights—would beep and flash and "talk" to anyone carrying it, indicating which sensor was tripped.

Thus, the Spy Tracker served as the perfect mobile early warning system. The team could determine when The Farmer was on the move anytime, day or night, without having to stare at the Stoneship control-room monitors twenty-four hours a day.

Lucas gathered up the branches of his fake scrub pine.

Crouching, he slowly waddled like a duck out into the clearing.

Up ahead a few yards grew a scraggly patch of Canadian thistle, about two feet high. When Lucas reached it, he pulled out one sensor pod and examined it by the light of his XP-4 Spy Pen. It was sensor I.

He pulled up the pod's black wire antenna and flicked the sensor I power switch from Off to On.

Then he placed the device in the thistle patch, hiding the pod, but carefully bending the antenna's red tip out into the clearing.

Now Lucas began his tracking map.

He opened the Spy Tracker case and plucked the black dry-erase marker from its slot. In the center of the green grid screen he drew a square, labeled it OLD FARM-HOUSE, and clearly marked its front door.

Are you still with us?

You aren't watching TV or running with scissors while reading this, are you?

Good.

Next, Lucas drew a small circle on the grid to the left of the house—a spot corresponding to the thistle clump where he had just planted sensor I. He labeled the circle SENSOR I and traced a line from the circle to the LED trip indicator light marked I.

Like this:

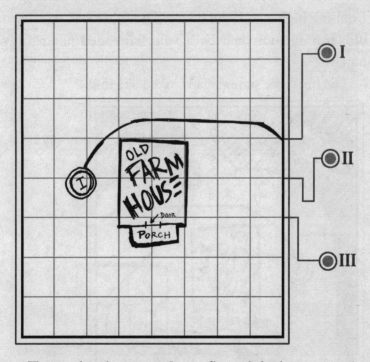

To test the placement, Lucas flipped the base station's power switch to No Sound mode. Then he waved his hand in front of the antenna. The sensor detected the motion, sent a signal to the base station—and the sensor I indicator light immediately started flashing. Bingo! It worked, by golly.

Lucas duck-walked in his fake scrub pine to two other locations on the edge of the clearing. At each he planted sensor pods and marked their locations on the base station map. One was near the dirt lane running from the highway to the house. The other was near an old, rotting tool shed by a wild, untended pumpkin patch.

The final base station map looked like this:

As Lucas carefully backed away from the last sensor placement, he felt his legs shaking.

Maybe it was all that duck-walking.

Or maybe he was just a *little* more scared than he knew.

Go Team Three

Cyril patted a pumpkin. "Hey, man," he said. "What are *you* doing out here?"

The pumpkin remained mute.

Then Cyril trained his Spy Night Scope on the pine bush creeping out of the clearing. His Phase Alpha job had been to keep a close eye on the farmhouse windows. No monstrous shadows had appeared—in fact, he saw no sign of any activity whatsoever.

So when Lucas reached the high weeds of the field, Cyril breathed a deep sigh of relief. Whew! Phase Alpha complete. He turned to move laterally for a better view of the south side of the house, where Phase Beta would now commence.

He took two steps in the darkness and fell.

"*Aaaaah!*"

For gosh sakes, Cyril, what now? said Lucas over the Spy Link.

"I keep tripping on vines!"

What vines?

Cyril scrambled to his feet. "The ones I keep tripping on."

Where?

"On the ground."

Huh, there's no ground vines over here.

Jake's voice entered the link. **Cyril's in that pumpkin patch. Maybe that's it. Cyril, can you check it out?**

Cyril got on his hands and knees and looked around. He couldn't see a thing. "I can't see a thing," he said.

Lucas said, **Use your XP-4 Spy Pen light, for gosh sakes!**

Cyril clapped one hand to his back pocket. "Oh, yeah," he said. "I forgot about that."

Cyril flicked on the light and trained the thin beam downward. All he could see was dirt and dead leaves and squashed pumpkin guts and a bunch of vines and then there was that strand of black cable. Nothing too interesting.

Wait a minute.

He got down close to the ground.

"I see a lot of vines," he said.

Jake said, **Okay, well, be careful then.**

Yes, said Lucas. **Here's an idea: Try lifting your huge honking feet when you walk.**

Cyril traced the beam along the strand of black cable. "Huh, well, that's funny," he said. "There seems to be, like, a strand of black cable running through the pumpkin patch." He laughed weakly.

Cable?

Cyril kept moving along the cable, stepping over vines and pumpkins.

"Yeah, cable."

You're sure?

Cyril gritted his teeth. "No. Now that I look at it more closely, I guess it could be a segment of the Alaska Pipeline."

Silence. Then: **Okay, so it's a cable.**

Where does it go? asked Jake.

Cyril followed the cable a few more yards. It seemed to be curving toward the Ridgeview Estates neighborhood. He said, "Looks to run toward that housing development over there."

Lucas gasped. **Maybe he's a cable thief!**

"A what?"

Maybe The Farmer is tapping into the cable relay station!

"Aha," said Cyril. "That would explain the multimillion-dollar stakeout back at Stoneship. This fiend hasn't been paying for his cable TV! Maybe he's even getting *free premium channels!*" He shook his head. "I tell you, given their response, I have new respect for the local cable company."

Lucas let out an exasperated sigh. **Cyril,** he said. **You can get more than TV through the connection. Ever hear of cable modem?**

"Hear of it?" said Cyril. "I invented it!"

Is it my turn yet? murmured a voice.

Wait! Who's that?

Go Team Four

Oh yeah, Lexi. We almost forgot.

Lexi crouched in a dry irrigation ditch about thirty yards south of the Old Farmhouse. Several Lexi-high clumps of thistle rose in the clearing, so a southern approach provided the best cover. Plus, the creepy, twisted willow tree hung over the porch there.

Jake said, Okay, let's forget the cable for now. Cyril, get back to your post.

"Roger. I'm heading back to—*aaaaah*!"

Jake ignored it. Lucas, be ready to move fast if we go to our Code Bravo contingency.

Roger, I'm ready.

"Good," said Jake. Okay, Go Team Four, you are clear for Phase Beta insertion.

"Thanks," said Lexi.

Be cool, woman, said Lucas.

Lexi smiled. It was dark and spooky and yet she felt light, almost weightless. Slobbering monsters lurked nearby, perhaps waiting for her to approach their lair. But Lexi felt a calm sense of confidence unlike any she'd ever felt before. It was amazing. Indeed, her response to Jake—"Thanks"—expressed *exactly* how she felt. Lexi felt pure gratitude for being chosen by her team to perform the most hair-raising part of the spy mission.

Lexi scrambled to the nearest thistle clump. Then to the next one. And the next one. Imagine a cross between a monkey and a jungle cat. Her crouching glide was so smooth, not a sound could be heard. Within seconds Lexi huddled at the base of the willow tree. Then she swung up into the low limbs.

It was a sight to behold.

Dude, those are some seriously mad skills, said Lucas in awe.

Of course, Lexi couldn't answer now. She lifted herself gently from branch to branch until she hung over the porch roof. It didn't look very sturdy, but she dropped lightly onto it anyway. Then she took two soft steps to the primary Phase Beta objective: a half-open skylight just above the porch.

The team had pinpointed this target in the planning stages. A careful scan of the house with the Spy Night Scope had revealed this as the only visible opening into the sanctum of the Old Farmhouse. Now Lexi pulled the bug—a small microphone—out of her jacket's inner pocket. She listened carefully at the hatchlike window. Nothing. Then she slowly peeled the paper cover off the adhesive back of the bug, slipped the device just inside the sill, and planted it.

Do you see what's coming yet?

Lexi blew twice, gently, on the mouthpiece of her Spy Link headset—a predesigned signal that indicated the bug was planted. Then she took one step down the porch roof toward the willow branches.

Creak!

She stopped. Then she took another step.

CREAK!

Lexi was not one to panic. She stood still. Then she reached very, very slowly for the nearest willow branch. She swung into the tree.

Everything looks good, said Jake. I've got the scope on the house. I see nothing. I think you're cool to come home, buddy.

And then Cyril spoke.

Whoa, he said. Looks like I broke this cable.

What?

When I tripped over it, like, the sixth or seventh time, said Cyril, I broke the cable.

There was a brief radio silence.

Then someone said, Uh-oh.

Jake, watching the porch, saw something that made his stomach flop.

The porch door was opening.

"Lexi!" said Jake quietly into his Spy Link. "Do . . . not . . . move."

As the door swung open, a dark, hulking figure stepped slowly out onto the deck.

Even with his night-vision scope, Jake couldn't make out the creature's face or body features because of the doorway's reddish backlit glow. It had wild, long hair on top, though the rest of it didn't look too monstrous. In fact, it looked human-sized.

Was it a man? Was it a monster?

Could this be the legendary Farmer?

Jake carefully whispered, "Go Team, report."

I see him, said Lucas. He's looking down, like, at the dirt.

This was true. The dark creature—let's call it the "Farmer"—was now crouching near the porch, examining the ground. Was he sniffing for intruders? Could he smell Lexi's tracks? Would he sniff and snort up the tree trunk into the branches, find poor Lexi, and extract her bowels in a gruesome, bloody gorefest?

Cripes! whispered Cyril. Now he's . . . looking at . . . me.

Yes, Jake could see that the Farmer was indeed staring out at the pumpkin patch. He slowly stood. Then he took a couple of slow, tentative steps toward Cyril's position.

"Don't panic," whispered Jake. "And don't move!"

As if I could.

Lucas suddenly said, Lexi, man, what the heck are you doing?

Jake swung his scope to view the tree. Lexi was slowly creeping along a thick branch. "Don't answer, Lexi," he said. "And stop moving! You're right above him. He'll hear you!"

And then it happened.

The sudden, ear-splitting crack of the willow branch pierced the quiet like a gunshot. Lexi had no time to grab another limb. As her body fell, smaller limbs snapped off the tree, sounding like a string of firecrackers in the silent night.

Beneath her, the Farmer jerked his head upward, his beastly hair swinging like a halo.

From their three respective locations, Lexi's partners froze in utter horror.

"Lexi!" cried Lucas.

And then something amazing happened.

Like an agile carnivore, the Farmer slid in one smooth and elegant motion beneath Lexi's hurtling body.

And caught her . . . perfectly.

"She's food!" yelled Cyril.

8

THE OMEGA LINK

On pure instinct Jake exploded out of his hiding place and sprinted toward the hairy creature holding Lexi. As he did, Lucas burst out of bushes to Jake's left, doing the very same thing.

Cyril, of course, was nowhere to be seen.

"Hey!" shouted Jake, waving his arms as he ran. "Hey, hey! Over here!" He hoped to distract the Monster enough to make it drop Lexi instead of feeding on her heart and spleen.

"*Woo woo woo woo woo!*" shrieked Lucas, also trying to distract the hideous gargoyle from its ghastly feast of flesh.

The Monster, eyes burning, turned to face them. But its other facial features remained shrouded in darkness. The Bixby brothers skidded to a halt—crouched, fists raised, ready to spring forward and rip what was left of Lexi from the beast's bloodthirsty jaws.

The savage just stared.

It heaved a breath.

Then it gently set Lexi on the porch and patted her head.

Bending sideways, it turned ominously to the Bixbys. Bravely Jake stepped closer to the freakish demon from the corrupted nether regions of depravity. The beast's head was turned, like its body. Its wild hair hung down in a tangle.

"Oh, great!" said the Monster. "I tweaked something in my back."

Jake tried to speak, but couldn't.

"Wow," said the merciless sentry of ruination. It pointed over at Lexi. "When I caught little Mowgli here, something went, like, *pop!*"

Jake and Lucas exchanged a look.

"Right here, dudes," it continued. "In my deltoid? By the shoulder blade? I don't suppose you have one of those instant heat-pack things on you? You know, where you squeeze it and you get, like, instant heat? It's like, in a little pack?"

Lucas, stunned mute, shook his head.

"No?" said the Monster.

It looked from boy to boy. After a moment, it stood up straight and stretched—snapping sounds, like knuckles cracking, could be heard. "Ho! Wow! *That's* better." Then the Monster turned to face Jake. After a few more seconds, he said, "So are you guys, like, a club of vocal-chord amputees?"

Jake had to swallow about 714 times before he could speak. (By coincidence, this is the exact number of home runs Babe Ruth hit in his lifetime.) His mouth had undergone a process called "de-salivation."

"No," he finally said.

"So who are you?"

"We're . . . a bunch of kids."

"Kids," repeated the Monster.

"Little kids, yeah."

"I see."

"Right," croaked Lucas. "You know?" He shrugged. "Like, little happy kids? Who, like, play?"

"Yeah, we were just, you know, giggling around out here," nodded Jake.

"You're giggling kids," said the huge flesh-craving brute.

"That's us!" said Lucas.

On the porch, Lexi looked hypnotized. She kept shaking her head, as if trying to shake brain-eating centipedes out of her ears.

"So were you spying on me?" asked the Monster.

This evoked a bunch of really lame forced laughter, so pathetic that everyone got embarrassed and refused to look at each other for fear they would break down, confess, and start sobbing.

Then: "Are you 'The Farmer'?" blurted out Lexi.

Everyone eyed Lexi. Both Bixby boys looked ill. The creature, however, looked amused.

"The 'farmer'?" he repeated.

"Yeah," mumbled Lexi.

Lucas chimed in. "Yeah, the guy who owns this farm and, like, kills people for sport."

The young man—for it was clear now that he was at least somewhat human—started laughing. "Whoa, dude!" he laughed. "That's a good one!" He kept laughing. His laugh sounded light and happy rather than, say, the laugh of a cannibal preparing to field-dress his dinner. In fact his laugh sounded a little bit relieved.

"So are you 'The Farmer'?" asked Lucas.

"No."

"Then who are you?"

"That's a really complex question."

"What's your name?" said Jake.

"Marco," said the man.

"Marco?" repeated Lucas. "As in, like, Marco Polo?"

"*Exactly* like that, except my last name isn't Polo." He scraped fingers through his wild hair. "In fact, it's totally different from Polo. My last name is entirely non-Polo, I have to admit."

A thought hit Jake. "Did we scare you?" he asked.

"Yes, actually."

Jake nodded and said, "I'm sorry. We . . . figured this old place was deserted. So we were just goofing around, you know—trying to scare each other. I'm Jake Bixby. This is my brother, Lucas, and that kid who dropped from the tree is Lexi."

"Hi, guys," said Marco.

"So, Marco, you don't own this farm?" asked Lucas, looking over at the Old Farmhouse.

"Nope. I rent." Marco shrugged. "It's cheap."

Lucas nodded and said, "Wow, it must be cool to live on a farm." Jake glanced over at Lucas, who was trying to sound distracted and uninterested. "So . . . how long have you been here?"

Marco started to speak, then stopped. He thought for a second. Then he said: "Well, I guess it's been about, oh, three weeks or so."

"Three weeks."

"That's what I said. Three weeks."

"Hmmm. Three weeks."

"Yes, that's . . . pretty much what I just said."

"Well," said Jake. "Again, sorry our noise scared you."

Marco said, "Actually, I didn't hear any noise." He pointed at a long strand of black cable running out from under the house. "Actually, something happened to my cable modem."

"*Oh, crap,*" came a voice from the pumpkin patch.

Marco looked out that way. He said, "More little happy kids?"

There was a pause. Then, slowly, Cyril shuffled into the clearing from the pumpkin patch. His shoulders hunched over so far they looked folded.

"It was me," said Cyril. "I'm the guy that broke your cable. I tripped over it, uh, once. And so then it just broke, like."

"Okay, whatever," said Marco, whipping a flashlight off a clip on his belt. "Show me the spot."

Cyril led everyone to the place where the cable was severed. As they walked, Marco pulled up his ragged flannel shirt, revealing a utility belt. Jake watched him closely. Marco really seemed like a normal, even nice, guy. When they reached the break, Marco expertly spliced the cable with tools from the belt.

"There," he said.

Lucas looked down with admiration. "Wow, that was fast," he said.

"I used to work for the cable company," said Marco.

Jake nodded and said casually, "What do you do now?"

"Student."

"Where?"

Marco turned to him and said, "Carrolton Community College. Hey, I gotta get back inside. I was in the middle of a chat session with my girlfriend and a couple of low-life buddies." He looked at Cyril. "If she breaks up with me, I'll have to kill you."

"I understand," said Cyril.

Marco's turn into the light revealed his face clearly for the first time. He was even younger than he sounded—maybe around twenty or twenty-five at the most, Jake figured. His hair was a wild matted mass of long dreadlocks, and he had big, dark eyes that receded deeply under a protruding forehead, like maybe his brain was too big. A girl might even find him handsome in a scary, unwashed sort of way.

"Can I ask you one more question?" asked Jake.

"Sure."

"What does 'The Farmer' look like?"

Marco stroked the stubble on his chin. "I'd have to say . . . old."

"Old? Like, ancient? Or just old?"

"Really old."

Cyril said, "Does he wear a hockey mask?"

Marco looked at him. "No," he said.

"Thanks, man."

Marco said good-bye and went back into his suddenly placid-looking farmhouse.

Team Spy Gear walked up the overgrown lane through peaceful fields buzzing with crickets. When they reached the old highway, they turned and followed it to Carrolton's safe, orderly suburbs. House after house after house, all alike, all neat, with trimmed lawns and lovely gardens. As they walked, nobody spoke what they all felt: Relief, yes, because they weren't brutally slain. But that wasn't all. Everyone also felt a distinct sense of disappointment.

That's right: disappointment.

The mystery had turned out to be so, well . . . *ordinary*.

The following Monday, Jake and Lucas, each lugging a backpack, staggered into Carlos Santana Middle School. Kids slogged up the central hall in a faceless mass, mooing like cattle being driven to the slaughterhouse. Grim teachers stood in their doorways clutching coffee drinks. The first bell rang. Children burst into tears. It was a typical morning.

"Mr. Bixby!" called one particularly foul-looking woman.

"Hello, Mrs. Burnskid," said Jake. "How are you this morning?"

"Step over here, please!"

Jake approached the frightening woman. He could easily picture *her* in a hockey mask.

"I did my math," said Jake. "All of it. Twice."

The woman just stared at him.

"Okay, so I'm thinking you have something else in mind?" said Jake. "Some other failing?"

In his ear, he suddenly heard: Ask if you can borrow her glass eye.

Jake slid his eyes sideways. Just down the hall, Cyril leaned against a locker, grinning like a lunatic. Both boys wore their Spy Link headsets, as did Lucas. And the link was active.

"What is that on your ear?" growled Mrs. Burnskid.

"On my ear?" said Jake. "Oh, this thing?" He touched his Spy Link headset. "It's, uh—"

"A music device?" snarled Mrs. Burnskid, revealing just a hint of pointy teeth.

"No no no, it's, uh—"

The new Math Tutor Deluxe, whispered Lucas in Jake's earphone.

"It's the new Math Tutor Deluxe," said Jake.

You got it to improve your math skills, said Lucas.

"I got it to improve my mad skills."

Math skills! repeated Lucas.

"I mean, my *math* skills, heh," said Jake. He glanced over at Lucas, who stood a respectful distance away, staring casually up at the ceiling.

Mrs. Burnskid glared at Jake with a look so piercing and horrifying, it could be duplicated only by actors wearing red contact lenses in vampire movies. She slowly held out her hand and said, "I do not like prevaricators, Mr. Bixby. I find that prevarication . . . *enrages* me."

Hi, guys! said Lexi suddenly in Jake's ear. **Can you hear me? Hello? Are you guys at school yet? I'm out on the playground. Hello? Hello?**

Lexi! said Lucas. **Go to Code Blue silence, like, immediately!**

Sure, said Lexi over the link. **What's going on?**

Lexi, you meatball, shut up! hissed Cyril.

Code Blue! said Lucas urgently. **Don't you remember what that means?**

It means shut up! shouted Cyril.

All this was going on in Jake's ear as he squirmed under the gaze of Agnes Marie Burnskid.

"Guys!" yelled Jake.

Mrs. Burnskid hissed, "Pardon me, Mr. Bixby?"

"Guys," said Jake. "Uh, *guys* . . . like me . . . need, like, extra math help. Especially in such an *exciting* and yet extremely challenging and, and yet of course *exciting* class such as your Math Difficulties course."

"Give it to me," said Mrs. Burnskid.

Jake said, "Okay, well, but it's attached to the, uh—"

The Algebra Base Unit! said Lucas.

"—the Algebra Base Unit," finished Jake.

Cyril! said Lucas. **Can you take this one? Like, quickly?**

Roger go, said Cyril.

Jake slowly unhooked the Spy Link earphone from his ear. He looked at it, then held it out. Mrs. Burnskid leaned in close to Jake, took the earphone, and put it to her ear. Jake tried very hard not to lean away in nauseous revulsion.

"I don't hear anything," she said with menace.

"Uh—"

Jake caught a glimpse of Cyril paging through a math textbook. Then he started to read something. Suddenly

Mrs. Burnskid raised her eyebrows. After a few seconds, she handed back the earphone.

"Well, Mr. Bixby," she said in a different tone.

"Yes?"

"I must say . . . I am surprised. And impressed."

"Gosh, thank you, Mrs. Burnskid," said Jake. "Thank you so much you wouldn't believe it."

"Maybe you'll actually matriculate into my Advanced Math Extremities course next year after all," she said.

"That would be . . . an honor I don't deserve," said Jake.

He slipped the headset back over his ear just in time to hear Cyril say, And can I have your glass eye, Mrs. Burnskid? I'd really like to put it in my nose and, like, totally freak out Megan Loudenbark. The urge to howl combined with the tension of the situation was too much for even Jake. He let out a blast that was half laugh, half snot explosion.

His hands clamped over his lower face in horror.

"Gesundheit," said Mrs. Burnskid. She smiled, turned, and lumbered into her classroom.

Cyril and Lucas walked up to Jake. They all watched the teacher go.

"Holy sheep heads," said Lucas.

"Thanks, guys," said Jake. "That was truly quick thinking." He turned to slap hands with his brother, and then looked at Cyril. "Now I know what it's like to be a news anchor."

Cyril just watched Mrs. Burnskid. He shuddered.

"From behind," he said, "that's one gruesome hunk of beef."

Team Spy Gear kept in touch via Spy Link throughout the morning.

The school day proceeded like a mind-numbing slideshow interrupted by short bursts of energy between periods, with kids clawing and trampling one another to reach their next classes.

At lunch the Spy Gear quartet met in a deserted corner of the playground. Lucas pulled a handheld Spy Supersonic Ear from his gadget pack and trained it on Sierra Foxworthy and her crowd. Yes, high-level electronic surveillance officially confirmed what Cyril had long suspected—"popular-girl" conversations sound very much like the twittering of demented parakeets.

Later, as the Bixby boys walked home with Cyril and Lexi, Lucas looked a little glum. Jake grabbed his brother's jacket and gave it a tug.

"What's the deal, man?" said Jake.

Lucas tried to smile. "I don't know," he said.

"Come on," said Cyril. He made his voice deep, like a CNN announcer. *"Search your feelings, Luke."*

Lucas sighed. Then he said, "I don't know." He slung his backpack from his shoulder and opened the flap. "Look at this stuff."

"Yeah?"

"It's so *astonishing*," said Lucas.

"Agreed."

"But . . . it's kind of a waste, isn't it?"

Jake nodded. He said, "You mean, because we're not using it to spy on anything that could, say, annihilate us."

"I guess that's it," said Lucas. "I mean, Sierra Foxworthy is scary and all. I'm pretty sure she could deploy squads of girls to execute some fairly nasty deeds and whatever."

"She already has."

"True."

Cyril said, "Eighth-grade girls shouldn't look like that."

"It is creepy," said Lexi.

"Sierra's made of wax," said Cyril. "And her crowd, dang. When they follow her around, it's like an Egyptian pyramid carving." He started walking with his arms and legs bent. "Oh, Cleopatra, goddess of the Nile, bestow us with your popularity!"

Jake laughed. "But I hear Sierra's getting braces," he said.

"No!" said Cyril. "That means the entire school will have oral wiring soon."

The mood lightened a bit. Then Jake said, "Okay. I say we head to Stoneship right now." He put a headlock on his brother and ruffled his hair. "Surely we can find something truly evil to spy on."

Back at Stoneship, the four used Cyril's cell phone to call their parents. They called their fathers instead of their mothers, and so instead of an hour of explanations and reassurances, the total, combined airtime elapsed was thirty-seven seconds.

"Now what?" asked Jake.

"Maybe we should go ask Marco some more questions," said Lucas.

"I don't know what those questions would be," said Cyril. "Except maybe, 'Marco, who does your hair? How do they get it to look like little snakes?'"

Jake stared at one of the monitors. He still had a funny feeling about the Old Farmhouse. But he had to admit that Marco seemed anything but sinister.

"I'd like to know just exactly *when* this surveillance station was in use," he said. "If we knew that, then maybe we could do some research and find out who was renting from The Farmer at that time."

"Or maybe The Farmer himself was living there," said Lucas.

"Could be."

Cyril sat at the main monitor and started tapping on the keyboard. The others gathered around him. For nearly an hour they tried various search tactics, brainstorming ways to hack into the Stoneship system, but to no avail. All four got so engrossed in the process that a small beeping sound from the nearby shelves almost went unheard.

But then Lexi said, "What's that?"

"What?" said Cyril.

"That beeping," said Lexi.

Now Lucas heard it. He followed the sound to the gadget shelf.

"It's the Omega Link," he said.

He picked it up. It stopped beeping.

"Well, that's interesting," he said. He put it back down. It started beeping again.

Lucas picked up the device again and brought it to the main console. He set it down. The beeping stopped again. But this time, something happened on the screen. Words! They slowly appeared, one letter at a time, as if being typed:

TYPE PROTOCOL CHARLIE STOP ENTER STOP 177893 STOP DATES

"What the monkey?" said Jake.

Cyril's eyes widened. He turned to the main monitor and typed the words "PROTOCOL CHARLIE." Then he pressed the Enter key. The screen turned deep blue with a small gray box in the middle. Then Cyril typed the number "177893." A page full of file icons appeared.

Cyril double-clicked on one of the icons. This opened a surveillance photo. The Old Farmhouse, in midday, with a black car parked in the lane behind it.

"Wow!" said Jake.

"Now what?" asked Lucas. He looked at the Omega Link. "It says, 'Dates.' Do you type in the word 'dates,' or what?"

"The files have dates," said Lexi.

Everyone looked at her.

"The files," said Lexi. "They, uh, have dates."

"Woman, you are a mad genius," said Jake, grinning.

Lexi blushed.

Sure enough, each file icon was dated—year, month, day.

"See how far back they go?" said Lucas. "Look! The first one on this page is dated May of last year! That's, what, almost a year and a half ago?" He gestured around the control room. "Do you suppose that's when this whole thing started?"

"Open it!" said Jake excitedly.

Cyril double-clicked on the oldest dated file icon and a photo popped onto the screen. It was a crisp, clear midday telephoto shot of an Old Farmhouse window. Someone was lifting up the window shade and peering out.

It was clearly Marco.

9

THE CABLE TRAIL

At this point you may want to review the ending of chapter 2. Go ahead. Take your time. We'll wait for you right here—here, at the end of this paragraph. Here, actually. Or maybe here.

Don't read the next paragraph until you've completed the review.

Stop reading ahead.

I said stop reading ahead.

You're doing it again.

Again, to repeat, what you want is chapter 2: "Meet the Bixbys"—the last few paragraphs. Just lick your finger and flip pages left to right, which is the "backward" direction in this book.

All right, I guess I'll do *all* the work, although I'm really disappointed in your lack of discipline. You may recall that at the end of chapter 2 we were in the Bixby living room at 44444 Agincourt Drive, finishing up a round of Clue with the Bixby family.

Okay, it was Monopoly. That was a test.

Anyway, Cyril and Lexi were there too. And—here's the important thing—Cyril had just indicated via meaningful looks that something back at Stoneship required the team's attention.

Of course, back in chapter 2 you had no idea what Stoneship was. You were entirely clueless! Ha! Remember how helpless you felt as we toyed with your emotions, manipulating you with sly references to some mysterious outfit known as "Team Spy Gear" and its highly important spy activities?

Remember that?

Now you know all that stuff. So let's come back to the present.

In fact, as you read this very sentence, the four kids are leaving the Bixby house, just as they were back in chapter 2 . . . way, way back before I took you into the past to see Team Spy Gear's origins. Oh look, now they're creeping through Stoneship Woods. Hey, they're entering the warehouse. Now they're gathering at the console monitor in the Stoneship control room.

"Check this out," says Cyril.

Since last Monday—when the Omega Link mysteriously provided passwords that unlocked the surveillance photo database—Cyril Wong has spent many bleary hours here at Stoneship, opening thousands of photo files. He's been searching for some clue to the nature of the Stoneship operation.

Photo after photo has revealed—well, not much. Most are shots of Marco engaged in various everyday tasks—sweeping, adjusting a window shade, talking on a cell phone, sitting on the porch, conjugating Latin verbs, and many other perfectly innocent-looking activities. Some might even call them "quotidian" tasks, although *you* wouldn't because you're just a kid.

"But then I found this folder," says Cyril.

The others watch as he moves the cursor over a folder icon tucked in a corner of the screen. He clicks once to highlight the folder's name: BATCH RED.

"Sounds important," says Jake.

"Open it!" says Lucas, bouncing on his toes.

"Actually," says Cyril, clicking open the folder, "the stuff in here isn't all that amazing. I mean, no pictures of Marco murdering people or committing heinous acts of carnage with a Bolivian machete or anything."

"Gee, that's too bad," says Jake.

"But check this out."

Cyril opens a file. It shows Marco drilling a hole in the Old Farmhouse's foundation, near the porch. Then Cyril opens more BATCH RED files. Each one shows Marco in the process of wiring the Old Farmhouse with the black cable—unwinding a spool of cable, stringing cable through the hole, running cable from the house through the pumpkin patch and then across the fields beyond.

"Why is that so interesting?" asks Jake.

"Good question."

"Looks pretty tame."

"Maybe," says Lucas. "But why would *Marco* be doing this?"

Cyril raises his hand and waves it around like an overeager student.

Lucas gives him a look. "Yes?"

"Uh, like," says Cyril, "uh . . . like, maybe because, like, he wanted . . . a cable connection?"

Jake's eyebrows go up. "Wait a minute," he says. He nods at Lucas. "I think I see where you're going."

Cyril rolls his eyes. "What's so unusual about some deadbeat dude rigging up his cable modem? I'm sure he spends all night online with about eighty-four other long-hair tattoo dudes, playing multiplayer mods of Gunship Rage! and Hematoma! instead of doing homework."

"Maybe," says Jake. "But why are these photos in a special folder?"

"And my point is, why would *Marco* wire his house?" says Lucas, still excited. "I mean, Cyril, when you order a connection from the local cable company, do they say, 'Sure, okay, here's a big honking spool of cable, good luck'?"

"Yes."

"No, they don't."

"Okay, but I'm going to keep saying yes."

"Why?"

"Because I hate being wrong."

Jake grins and whacks Cyril lightly on the back of the head.

"Okay, okay," says Cyril. "So maybe I admit this is unusual. But still, is laying cable, like, a federal crime?" He gestures at the surveillance technology around the control room. "I mean, what can you do with a cable modem that attracts attention like this?"

Jake notices Lexi, who seems deep in thought.

"What are you thinking, little woman?" asks Jake.

Lexi starts and looks up.

Lucas turns to his best buddy. He says, "Yo homes, what you got?"

Lexi says, "Maybe he's a hacker."

There is a moment of silence, one of those poignant ones where you can almost hear everyone's thoughts clacking into place.

"*Of course!*" shouts Lucas.

Cyril looks up at Jake and nods, his hair bouncing like a wire sombrero. "Now *that* makes sense," he says.

"Yes, it does."

Cyril says, "And dude, maybe he's one of those really *bad* ones."

"What do you mean?" asks Jake.

Cyril looks back at the monitor, which displays the photo file of Marco unspooling cable out into the farm's ragged fields. "Maybe he's, like, one of those guys you hear about who try to hack nuclear launch codes."

"Why would he want those?"

"To nuke stuff!"

"Like what?"

"I don't know," says Cyril. "Maybe the place where they grow Brussels sprouts."

Jake bursts out laughing.

"Hey, it's not funny," says Cyril. "I happen to *like* Brussels sprouts."

For a few minutes the four speculate on what kind of hacker Marco might be. Maybe he's one of those free-loaders who tap into corporate servers so they can store a few terabytes of MP3 music files at no cost. Maybe he's a fired worker who's mad at his old company, or an Internet vandal who just gets a thrill out of messing up Web sites.

Or maybe it's more serious.

Maybe Marco is stealing government secrets or money or credit-card information.

Lucas walks over to the gadget shelves. "Answer me this question," he says, picking up a pair of high-tech Eye-Link Communicator headsets. "Who could afford a surveillance pit like this, with all these superprimo gadgets?"

Cyril answers, "Somebody with a lot of resources and money, obviously."

"Like the FBI?" asks Jake.

Lucas shakes his head. "No, if cops or the FBI were doing this spying, they wouldn't just leave all this expensive stuff behind."

"Good point," says Cyril.

Lucas looks around and says, "So maybe it was, like, a private operation, like maybe some big-shot corporation, or maybe an Internet security consulting firm *working* for a big corporation."

"But still, why would they abandon this place?" asks Jake.

Lucas just shrugs. There is a moment of silence. Nobody has an answer to this question. Then Lexi leans in closer to the photo of Marco on the screen.

She says, "Where's he going in this picture?"

Lucas stares at the photo too. "Out into the fields, looks like."

Lexi looks over at Lucas. "But why?"

Lucas says, "Probably running cable to one of the relay boxes in the Ridgeview Estates neighborhood."

"But he's going *away* from the neighborhood," says Lexi. "In the opposite direction."

Lucas squints harder at the photo. "Gee, he is, isn't he?" Then he says, "Hey, Cyril, are there more photos in this series?"

"Yeah," says Cyril. "But they just show Marco rolling

his spool of cable out of sight." He clicks open a few more photo files. "See? He just sort of disappears into the weeds, laying cable."

"I wonder where that cable goes?" asks Lexi. "Geez, maybe we should find out."

Jake wraps an arm around Lexi's shoulder. "Sister, you are a treasure," he says.

"Thanks, Jake."

"Yeah, we love you, man," says Lucas.

They whack hands and Lexi starts laughing, a rare sight. Pretty soon, all the kids are cackling like wild roosters. Why? Because thrilling, dangerous work lies ahead. *And Team Spy Gear is back in business!*

"Okay, guys," calls Jake.

Everybody stops laughing and looks at him.

He says, "Time for some more fieldwork."

Woo-hoo! The hooting and hollering starts right up again.

Because let's face it, folks:

Spying on people is beastly fun and about the coolest thing there is.

THE DARK MAN

Cyril adjusts his headset. He stares at the main console screen in the Stoneship control room. "Go Team, test test," he says. "Do you read me?" Jake, Lucas, and Lexi all respond. "Roger, Go Team, now let's try voiceless," says Cyril. "All units: Go to Eye-Link Communicators."

He flips a switch on the console next to a display labeled VOX CHANNEL. Then he types "STEALTH TEST X ALL UNITS REPORT."

After a few seconds text messages start appearing on the screen:

1 (JAKE): . . . GO TEAM ONE HERE X DO YOU READ? . . .

3 (LEXI): . . . HI CYRIL THIS IS THREE . . .

2 (LUCAS): . . . TWO HERE . . .

Cyril smiles. The tactical plan calls for him to direct operations from Stoneship. His job: monitor camera views and provide reports to his field team. He's happy to be here and not in the field—although it is a bit scary to be alone in an abandoned warehouse. For example: Was that a sound he just heard?

Cyril stands. Nervously he leans forward to the big window overlooking the warehouse floor.

From up here Cyril can see through the open cargo door below. Outside, the Stoneship loading dock glimmers in the ashen moonlight. The forest beyond is as black as oblivion.

Cyril shivers.

He sits back down and types a response to his Go Team.

Doing so, he just misses seeing a dark shadow drift like an apparition across the cargo doorway.

Jake crouches at the split-rail fence around the Old Farmhouse property. Suddenly glowing words appear like magic, floating before his right eye:

4 (STONESHIP): . . . ALL COMLINKS CONFIRMED? . . .

Jake turns to Lucas and Lexi, who crouch beside him. Both nod. Jake nods back. Then, with his right forefinger, he taps alphabet keys on a small keypad strapped to his left wrist, typing "AFFIRMATIVE." He presses the keypad's Send button.

"*Geez,* I love this stuff!" shouts Lucas. "It's beyond beastly."

"*We're voiceless!*" barks Cyril.

"Right," says Lucas. "Sorry."

The three-man Go Team—Jake, Lucas, and Lexi—all wear Eye-Link Communicator headsets in addition to their standard, voice-activated Spy Link walkie-talkies. Each headset has an eyepiece with an inset liquid crystal display (LCD) miniscreen that shows text messages sent from teammates. This way, a field team can switch to voiceless communication if necessary.

Roger, Go Team, let's go back to voice link, commands Cyril's voice in their Spy Link earphones.

"Okay," says Jake. He turns to the younger kids. "Ready to go, Lexi?"

Lexi perks up, and nods with a hint of excitement. Even in the dark you can see a glint in her eyes. Lexi was born to face physical danger, you see. In another life she'd be the first commando out of the landing barge onto Omaha Beach.

Lucas taps Lexi on the shoulder. "Dude, you sure you're okay to go solo again?" he asks.

Lexi answers, "*Oh* yeah."

"Okay." Lucas looks at Jake. "Let's deploy."

Jake nods. He says, "Stoneship?"

Coast clear, says Cyril. Marco's in-house. I've seen his shadow two or three times, but no sign of outside activity.

"Roger, thanks," says Jake. Then he gestures toward the weed field with a rolling finger sign. "Okay, kids, let's go."

Cyril taps nervously on the console desktop.

His eyes move from monitor to monitor, scanning all four camera views of the Old Farmhouse. As he glances at the south-side view, he catches a hint of shadow on the reddish glow of a window shade—the one overlooking the porch.

"Go Team, I have movement," he says, leaning close to the monitor. He watches carefully. After a few seconds the shadow moves away from the window. Cyril relaxes. "All clear again," he says.

Keep those updates coming, dude, crackles Jake's voice in his ear.

We're sending in the scout, says Lucas. **Mad skills, dude. Good luck.**

Okay, says Lexi.

Be careful this time, Frodo, says Jake.

Okay, says Lexi.

Cyril, listening, can hear the excitement in their voices, and he actually feels a twinge of regret. But it passes quickly. Glancing at the monitor, he casually notes the huge willow overhanging the farmhouse porch. As he scans the scary old tree, a flashback of Lexi falling through its branches flickers across Cyril's inner eye, like a vision. He frowns. Something tugs at his memory. What is it? Something wants to be remembered, but Cyril can't quite conjure it up.

Cyril can hear Jake breathing hard.

These weeds are nasty, man, Cyril hears Jake say. **Isn't that the pumpkin patch over there?**

Yeah, that's it, says Lucas.

Beep! Beep! Beep!

Cyril taps on his earphone. He says, "Do you hear that?"

Hear what? asks Jake.

Beep! Beep! Beep!

"There it is again," says Cyril. "Hear it?"

What?

"That beeping!"

Lucas, Lexi, says Jake. **Do you hear beeping?**

No.

Nope.

Beep! Beep! Beep!

We don't hear beeping, Cyril, says Jake.

Cyril presses the Mute button on his Spy Link headset and listens. All is quiet for a second. Then, faintly: *Beep! Beep! Beep!* He turns in the direction of the sound.

Lucas nearly cheers when he hears that the Omega Link is alive again. He loves that thing, is why. It's such a supersecret gizmo that nobody can figure it out. To a guy like Lucas, that makes it the Wicked Sweet Mother of All Gadgets.

"Pick it up, Cyril!" he whispers.

Why?

"Remember last time it beeped?" says Lucas. "It has information. Dude, pick it up."

Jake says, "He's right, Stoneship." He surveys the pumpkin patch quickly as he speaks. "Pick it up."

All right.

After a few seconds of silence, Lucas can't stand it anymore. "What's happening?" he hisses.

Nothing.

"Nothing?"

It just stops beeping when I pick it up.

"What's on its display screen?"

Nothing.

"Rats!" says Lucas. Then he remembers: "Wait! Cyril, set it down on the console. Just like last time. Put it by the central monitor."

More silence.

"Cyril, dang it!"

What?

"What the monkey is happening?"

Well . . . , says Cyril. **Uh. Wait. Oh, there it goes.**

Lucas pumps his fist and says, "*Yes!* Can you be more specific?"

The display reads, uh . . . 'Vox plant channel seventeen.' There is a pause. Then Cyril adds: **If you can tell me what that means, I'll give you four crackers.**

Lucas jumps up and starts pacing around pumpkins, hands clasped behind his back. "Vox plant?" he muses. "Vox is voice. Voice something? A plant? A talking plant? I don't get it."

Jake grabs his brother's arm and pulls him down. He

says, "Hey, bro, do your brainstorming out of sight and just a *little quieter*, okay?"

"Or wait! No! Wait! I got it!" Lucas is so excited he jumps back up again. He slaps his forehead hard and says, "Holy crud! Are we stupid, or what?"

"What do you mean?" asks Jake, yanking his brother back down among the pumpkins. "You think it's a talking plant?"

"No no no! Not a talking plant! A *listening* one!"

Suddenly words appear on their Eye-Link Communicator headsets:

. . . YES IT IS STILL THERE . . .

Jake looks over at the Old Farmhouse and says, "Lexi? Is that you?"

. . . YES . . .

"*What's* still there?"

. . . THE BUG . . .

Jake's jaw drops open. "Good gosh," he says. "The bug! The one Lexi put in the skylight!"

"Exactly!" says Lucas. "That's what I was trying to say. That's the *vox plant*. We totally forgot about it. What a bunch of bonehead spies we are! Where are you, Lexi?"

. . . IN THE TREE . . .

"Wow." Lucas and Jake exchange a look. "You are one fast spy there, dude."

... I CAN SEE IT FROM HERE ...

"Excellent!" says Lucas.

... SEE MARCO TOO ...

"What's he doing?" asks Jake.

... TALKING ON CELL PHONE ...

"Wow, Lexi, stay voiceless," says Lucas. "You don't want him to hear you. Cyril, do you hear all this? You need to—"

"Absolutely already done, dude," says Cyril, punching buttons like a maniac on the Stoneship console. He turns the Channel Select dial next to the Vox Channel's digital display. "Okay, channel seventeen," he says, scrolling through numbers on the display. "Here it is."

Suddenly Marco's voice echoes thinly in the console speakers. Are you threatening me? he says.

"Yeah, sounds like he's on the phone, all right," says Cyril. "Listen, I think I can route it into our Spy Link channel." He punches a few more buttons. Then: "Aha! Here we go!"

Look, man, I said I was in, crackles Marco, sounding like an old radio broadcast. I launch in exactly thirty-three minutes.

"Crickets!" exclaims Cyril. "Launch? What does that mean?" No answer. "What do you think, guys?" No sound. "Go Team? Hello? Hello? Jake?"

Nothing.

"Uh-oh," says Cyril.

He starts punching more buttons.

As Cyril frantically tries to reconnect to his team, a dark figure is slinking into the warehouse below. In the darkness, everything is very dark. All we can see is the dark outline of a man. Everything else is quite unlit and pretty gosh-darned dark.

We'll call this intruder . . . the "Dark Man."

Let's go down there, shall we? Don't be afraid. This is just a story, remember. No evil can arise from these pages to harm you, except of course at midnight, or if you foolishly leave the book open to this page and light a black candle and speak The Sumerian Curse.

Anyway, the dark figure drifts slowly beneath the control room and stops. The haunting chords of Mozart's Requiem in D Minor, a really very scary piece of music, can be heard in the author's mind as the Dark Man lights a match. But his hat blocks the small flame's glow. We cannot see his face. Is it disfigured? We can't tell, because of the stupid hat. Now puffs of smoke curl around the hat's dark brim.

The match goes out.

Darkness rules again.

Well—except for the pulsing glow of the Dark Man's cigarette. And then, well, there's that little flame on his sleeve, too.

He slinks forward a few more steps. Then, smelling smoke, he looks around.

He sees his burning sleeve.

The Dark Man tries to back away from the flame, but of course he cannot, because he's wearing the very coat to which the sleeve is attached. Plus, as he backs away, he trips over a shipping pallet.

His fall is swift and silent.

Sprawled on his back, the Dark Man starts waving the burning arm around, and though it looks really cool, the motion merely fans the flames. Next he rolls over and over and over, and the graceful motion of the whipping fire looks like something in a spectacular Las Vegas circus act, but unfortunately, the guy's arm is still on fire. Finally he tears off the coat and starts beating it unmercifully on the ground.

The fire dies. Darkness reigns again.

The odor of smoke is sickening, though. Whew! What a putrid smell!

Jake and Lucas Bixby call for Cyril again and again, but get no answer. They try typing messages on their Eye-Link Communicators. Nothing works.

"He cut us off," says Jake.

"Great!" says Lucas.

"Lexi, are you still with us?" calls Jake.

The word "YES" appears in the Eye-Link eyepieces of both Bixby boys.

"Okay, good," says Jake. "So let's stick to the plan, Go Team. Lexi, do your thing, kid. Lucas, let's find that cable."

Each Bixby boy whips out his XP-4 Spy Pen and flicks on its penlight. They get down low in the pumpkin patch, looking for Marco's cable. As Jake searches, he finds himself worrying about Cyril. They've been best friends since the first moment they met over clay activities at The Lucky Exclusive Preschool. They'd survived Rocketry Summer Camp explosions and attacks by deranged percussionists in KinderMusik classes. In fact Jake couldn't think of many important moments in his life that didn't somehow include Cyril.

"Here it is!" calls Lucas.

"Good job," says Jake. "Cyril, are you back online? Cyril? Dude?"

Lucas hears it—the thing—inside his brother's voice. He pats Jake's arm and says, "Hey, he's all right. I'm sure he just tripped and broke a cord or something."

"Yeah," says Jake.

Lucas says, "If he detonated anything, we would have heard it."

Jake grins.

The brothers follow the black cable away from the house into the fields. About one hundred yards out, a clump of scruffy cottonwood saplings rise above the weeds. The cable leads right into the small thicket.

Jake pushes through branches into a small open

area. In this clearing sits a satellite dish—a big one, at least ten feet across.

"Aha!" says Lucas.

"So Marco's wireless," says Jake.

"Obviously," says Luke.

Jake looks up at the sky. "Do you suppose he has his own satellite up there?"

Lucas laughs. "I wouldn't be surprised," he says, peeking upward.

Guys? Guys? Can you hear me now? It's Cyril.

"Yes, Stoneship, we copy!" says Jake, very much relieved.

Cyril has discovered that he can connect to his Go Team on channel 1 *or* to the bug transmission on channel 17—but not to both at the same time. He quickly explains this to the Bixbys.

"I'm going to flip back and forth," he says. "Marco is having a very lengthy and interesting phone conversation. Out!"

Cyril rolls the Channel Select dial back to 17 and listens to Marco again.

. . . if everyone is coordinated, the attack goes well," he says, sounding irritated. **"Look, Viper, threats don't work on these guys. Or on me, for that matter. The hacker community is, well, it's a lot of guys who hate authority. It's based on—**

As Marco speaks these words, Lexi watches him through the farmhouse skylight. The hairy hacker stops in midsentence, and an unmistakable look of horror spreads across his face.

"How did you get that information?" says Marco. "How can you—"

His face grows pale and drawn.

"You wouldn't dare!" he says weakly.

The response on the other end of the line forces Marco to slump into a chair.

Then he says: "You, you— —" And he calls the person a very bad name. Finally, Marco swivels to his computer monitor which sits on a rickety old desk. He says, "We go in twenty-three minutes."

Marco pushes the End button on his cell phone. He stares at the device for a second. Then he hurls the phone against the far wall.

Pieces shatter everywhere.

Lexi, stunned, inches a bit closer to the window.

Cyril hears all of this. He switches channels again.

"Something's up, Go Team!" he says excitedly. "And I mean, like, right now! Marco's doing something bad in about twenty minutes—some kind of attack, sounds like—and he has partners."

. . . DOING SOMETHING ONLINE . . .

"Can you see it, Lexi? What's on his computer screen right now?"

. . . TOO FAR AWAY . . .

"You need to find out." Cyril thinks. "Dang. We need to get Marco out of there. Jake?"

Right, says Jake quickly via Spy Link. **Working on a diversion plan here.**

"Hurry!"

Lucas, what would happen if we, like, gave this dish a twist?

Good question, answers Lucas.

Would it cut off his satellite link?

Cyril jumps in and says, "Maybe, or at least change his dish parameter settings enough to set off an alarm or something. That might lure him outside to check the dish. Lexi, where's Marco?"

. . . AT COMPUTER TYPING STUFF . . .

"Give that dish a twist, boys!" says Cyril, juiced with excitement.

But then he hears a sound. It's a bad sound.

He turns to face the sound.

The floor hatch leading down to the ladder slowly slides open.

Kids, at this point you may want to stop and explain to your parents what's going on.

All this quick flipping between characters can be confusing to older readers, so your mom or dad might have questions. Remember: They've consumed a lot of espresso drinks over the past fifteen or twenty years. Be patient with them. Talk slowly.

Okay, let's see now. Where were we?

Oh yeah. Cyril was about to confront the Dark Abyss of Calamity, face to face.

I'm sure it will be interesting, but we'll get back to that in a minute—or if Cyril gets killed or maimed, we might just skip it altogether. Anyway, first let's check in on Lexi.

Through the skylight Lexi watches Marco click things on his computer screen. Then Marco freezes. He stares at his monitor. Then he grabs two fistfuls of his hair and starts cursing so badly we'll have to come take your book away if you guess what he's saying.

"No!" he screams. "Not now!"

He leaps to his feet and bashes through the door into the yard. From the porch roof Lexi sees him sprint through the pumpkin patch into the darkness.

"He's coming!" says Lexi.

It's okay, we're away, says Jake quietly. Then: Yep, I can hear him cussing a hundred yards away.

Move fast! says Lucas to Lexi. And be smart, dude! We'll tell you when he's returning.

Lexi scurries like a spider through the skylight, lowering herself onto a nearby bookshelf and then to the floor. She hustles over to Marco's computer. A bunch of unreadable gobbledygook is scrolling down the monitor. Suddenly an instant message window pops on to the screen.

Then another. And another.

"He's getting a bunch of instant messages," says Lexi breathlessly.

Read them to us! whispers Jake over the Spy Link.

Lexi reads: "Servers five to eleven all down. The signature line reads 'MasterHack.'"

Another message appears. Lexi reads: "Virginia down. Blue Sector servers under attack. Signature is 'Hackberry Farm.'"

Then another pops up. Lexi reads: "'Polo, you there? Four more and we kill the whole thing. History!' The signature: 'KillTheNet.'"

Kill the Net? whispers Lucas in momentous tones. **My gosh. I think this is a coordinated attack on the Internet. They're trying to bring the whole honking thing down!**

"Is that bad?" asks Lexi.

Lucas ignores this question. **Lexi, is there anything else you can see on-screen? Anything that looks even remotely important?**

Lexi grabs the mouse and clicks on something up in a corner. A long e-mail maximizes across the desktop. "He's got a big e-mail here from someone," says Lexi, scrolling down. "It's signed 'Viper.'" She thinks a moment. "Hey, that's who Marco was talking to on the phone."

Lucas whispers even more quietly: **Lexi, he's at the dish. Listen carefully. To take down the entire Internet you have to crash all thirteen servers that shape its architecture. If** one or two survive the attack, the Net slows considerably, but doesn't die.

Jake says, Dang! Sounds like his little group of hackers has crashed most of them already. And Marco's the missing link, no doubt. He probably has two or three servers targeted from here.

Lexi stares at the computer. "What should I do?"

Pull the plug! says Lucas. Rip out any wires or cords you can find! Hurry! Go, like, totally destructomatic, girl!

First Lexi whips out her Spy Camera—a pair of sunglasses with a minicamera mounted on the frames. She snaps two quick shots of the e-mail, then gets to work. As Lexi rips and tears and bashes things, she can't help it: She smiles. Admit it: Isn't this something *you've* always wanted to do too? Like, go totally postal on your computer setup?

Lexi, he's done with the dish, whispers Jake urgently. He's heading back to the house!

Did you trash his rig? asks Lucas.

"Yes," says Lexi, looking over her work with great satisfaction.

Severely?

"Oh yes."

Then get out of there, fast!

Lexi clambers quickly up the bookshelf to the skylight. As in every good spy tale, she pulls herself through the opening just as Marco bursts through the door.

In her ear, Lexi hears Cyril shouting: Who is it? Who's there?

Jake and Lucas meet up at the satellite dish. As they do, they hear Cyril shouting too.

"Cyril, what's up?" says Jake.

Cyril sounds sick. He whispers, Somebody . . . opened . . . the hatch.

Jake and Lucas look at each other. They are a good mile from Stoneship. Even running full speed, they'd have to flounder through thick weeds and forest on the way. It would take at least ten or twelve minutes to reach Cyril in the warehouse.

"Cyril," says Jake. "Stay calm. Do you hear anything?"

There is a pause. Then: No.

"Look through the control room windows," says Jake. "Do you see anything?"

Another pause, then: No.

"Can you sneak over to the hatch and peek down?" asks Jake.

A really long pause. Then: No.

"Come on, dude," says Jake. "You can do it."

Suddenly red words appear before Jake's eyes:

. . . MARCO IS INSANE . . .

"Lexi?" says Lucas. "Are you out?"

. . . YES AND MARCO IS LIKE HOWLING . . .

Suddenly Jake and Lucas can hear it too. Marco is

indeed howling. It's a thing to hear, let me tell you. Rage like that could inflate blimps.

"Jake, he's going to look for a perpetrator!" says Lucas suddenly. "Lexi, I think you're in danger. Where are you?"

No response.

"Lexi?" calls Lucas loudly.

"Cyril?" calls Jake loudly.

Nothing. Not a sound.

⑪

DARKNESS!

Oh yeah . . . Cyril

What's up with that guy?

Well, a lot, actually. For example: Right now, he's surrounded by a total blackout in the Stoneship control room. Yes, the lights are out. Someone has cut the power. The console is dead too. Monitors, displays, everything—dead.

And Cyril hears something moving up the ladder. Very, very slowly.

Cyril tries to speak. But his voice is crushed, as if cold icy fingers are mangling his larynx. Now he hears the *swish!* of the dark murderer's cloak as he emerges from the unseen hatch. In the dead silence Cyril hears a rattling breath and then small tapping sounds on the floor— perhaps drips of drool as the brutal predator approaches, hungry for homicide. Or maybe not, but gosh, it doesn't sound good, does it?

Plus there's a really bad smell. Like something burned recently.

Cyril tries to gather his wits, which are currently scattered over Baffin Bay, north of the Arctic Circle between Canada and Greenland. But as he hears light footsteps approach, Cyril's mind can see only gruesome images of medieval gore.

Mom's right, he thinks grimly. *Videogames have warped my mind, and clearly portend the decline of civilization into chaos.*

Boy, is it dark in here, or what?

Really, it's so dark that not even the author can see a darn thing.

Cyril, who sits in the console chair, can hear the intruder pass swiftly and surely toward the gadget shelf. Why? What cruelty is this? Is he just toying with his prey? Or does he seek some high-tech torture gizmo? Some grim, electronic Doom Device?

But then Cyril hears a painful smacking sound— somewhat like the sound a man's shin makes when it strikes the corner of a galvanized-steel shelving unit.

Then Cyril hears a yelp of pain.

Then Cyril hears a series of thuds, not unlike the sound of one shoe hitting the floor again and again as if, say, a man was hopping on one foot.

Then there is a moment of silence.

The moment seems to last years.

And Cyril, believe it or not, starts tapping his foot. He's actually getting kind of bored, sitting here, waiting for his destruction.

Boy, this is lasting forever, isn't it? All this hearing of stuff, with no seeing? Wow.

Hang in there. It's almost over.

Okay, so *then* Cyril hears a scrape, followed by a small beep—as if some device has been activated—followed by several more beeps, not unlike the dialing sounds of a touch-tone phone.

Here Cyril has the presence of mind to reach over to the dark, powerless console, feel for the plug of his Spy Link headset, pull it out, and then plug it into his battery-powered belt unit. Now he can contact his teammates again. Not that it would do any good.

In his ear, he hears:

Cyril?

Lexi?

Cyril?

Lexi?

Cyril?

Lexi?

He unplugs the link again.

He can't bear the thought of hearing his buddies call his name at the moment of his assassination. Besides, he can't hear the killer's movements with all that chatter in his ear.

And then, guess what?

Something miraculous happens.

Footsteps move away from the gadget shelf . . . heading back to the hatch!

Cyril's eyes, which have adjusted a bit during these interminable weeks of darkness, see a vague dark shape descend into the hole. He hears the raspy breath of a man laboring down the ladder. Cyril takes a couple of steps toward the hatch. He hears something crash below. Things fall. He hears a cry of pain. More things fall.

In a rare flash of courage, Cyril rushes to the gadget shelf.

His hands fumble blindly over items until he finds what he seeks—a Spy Night Scope! Quickly he hurries to the window overlooking the warehouse floor, lifting the scope to his eyes as he goes.

The greenish, hazy night-vision view reveals the sight of a huge, ominous shape standing like a dark angel in the cargo doorway. For a brief second the figure looks up toward Cyril.

Then it turns . . . and limps painfully out of sight.

Seconds later, the power returns.

Meanwhile, back at the farm, Jake and Lucas try desperately to save Lexi. The two Bixbys crouch in the pumpkin patch. Not far away, on the Old Farmhouse porch, Marco is howling obscenities into the night sky. Just above him, on the porch roof, Lexi hunkers.

Lucas pulls two Spy Night Scopes out of his gadget backpack and tosses one to Jake. They quickly train their scopes on Marco.

"Don't move, don't make a sound," whispers Lucas over the Spy Link.

"Yeah, hang tight, Lexi," says Jake quietly.

"Jake, should we lure Marco away from the house?" asks Lucas.

"Maybe as a last resort," says Jake tensely. "Let's not get ourselves caught—not yet, anyway."

On the porch Marco grows quiet.

It's hard to see his facial expression in the Spy Night Scope haze, but it appears that something, some idea, has suddenly hit the hacker. Jake watches in growing concern as Marco slowly turns to face the willow tree. Then he looks upward.

"He's looking up the tree," says Lucas breathlessly.

Jake nods. "He remembers Lexi's fall the other night."

Marco seizes a shovel leaning against the porch railing. He steps off the porch.

"Jake, he's gonna see Lexi up there!" says Lucas.

"Get ready to move," says Jake tersely.

Marco keeps backing away from the house until he

can surely see the dim outline of Lexi's figure on the porch roof. But it's dark. Marco moves sideways a few steps for a better look.

Then, finally, he shouts, "Is that you up there, kid?"

Nervous? Well, you should be.

Marco takes a step closer to the porch. "If it is, you're one dead little dude."

"Stay where you are," says Jake calmly.

But then, slowly, Lexi stands. She rises up to her full height—a towering four feet, three inches tall. Then, with great flair, she sticks her thumbs in her ears and waggles her hands at Marco. She also makes a noise that sounds like this:

Gobbledy gobbledy gobbledy gobbledy gobbledy!

"Lexi, what are you—," begins Lucas.

He can't catch me, says Lexi. And she chuckles. Yes, you heard right. Chuckles.

Hi, guys! bursts Cyril's voice into the transmission. I'm back. Hey, guess what? I'm alive! Nobody murdered me. And geez, the weirdest thing happened—

"Cyril!" hisses Lucas, watching Lexi scamper atop the Old Farmhouse roof as Marco chases her around the corner, shrieking and waving the shovel in a black fury.

Yeah?

"We have a situation here!"

Yes! It's incredible, really. I mean, I was just sitting there in the dark when suddenly—

"Lexi's in big trouble!"

No, I'm not, laughs Lexi. This is fun!

"Fun?" says Jake. "Dude, he's trying to spear you with a spade!"

Jake and Lucas prepare to charge. But as the scene unfolds in all its goofy green majesty through their Spy Night Scopes—well, it seems Lexi is right. Marco, clomping around corners in clunky Doc Martens boots, could never possibly catch their agile chum.

Uh, guys, interrupts Cyril.

"Not now, Cyril!"

But listen, I think—

"Cyril, we're busy!"

I know, but—

And then the bad thing happens.

Look, you knew it was coming because this is a spy book, and spies always get into dangerous situations. In this case, Lexi gets a little too tricky for her own good. As she hops nimbly over a stovepipe protruding through the roof, she lands on a loose shingle. Footing lost, she slips, and slams backward onto her tailbone and slides down the slanted roof.

Just as she goes over the edge, Lexi manages to twist sideways and grab the rain gutter.

Now she hangs by one hand from the gutter, dangling

like a trout on a line . . . just as Marco rounds the corner.

Jake and Lucas rise from the pumpkin patch, poised and ready.

Marco runs up underneath Lexi.

He wields the spade like a baseball bat. There is an unbearably tense pause. But then . . . he drops the shovel. Staring at Lexi, Marco shakes his head and takes a deep breath. Then he says, "Dude, you just, like, totally ruined my life."

Lexi twists, rotating to face Marco.

Cyril cuts in on the Spy Link channel and says, Okay, Lexi, I got you back on visual sighting and—whoa, that doesn't look good, dude!

Marco steps closer to Lexi. He reaches for the dangling girl. Nearby, Jake and Lucas prepare to sprint to Lexi's rescue.

Suddenly the Spy Tracker base unit beeps in Lucas's backpack, and the voice alarm starts chirping, "Sensor three! Sensor three! Sensor three!"

Lucas freezes. "Sensor three?"

Jake looks around and says, "Where's that?"

Lucas spins to his left and says, "It's right over there, at the head of the lane—"

I've got incoming! yells Cyril in their ears. Duck, people!

Jake and Lucas drop into the pumpkins. In a sudden explosion of sound, three big black automobiles, identical, headlights dimmed, thunder past the pumpkin patch into the clearing.

On the far side of the house, Marco spins in the direction of the engines' roar. Terrified, he sprints around the house, away from the sound. Lexi seizes the rain gutter with her free hand and manages to pull herself back onto the roof—just as the cars fishtail around the corner, kicking up dark dust clouds, and then screech to a halt.

Black car doors fly open. Six men in black suits and night-vision goggles leap out.

Holy ham hocks! says Cyril. **It's the cavalry!**

"Jake, Marco's coming this way!" says Lucas.

It's true. Marco is making a mad dash into the pumpkin patch. The dark-suited agents round the first corner of the house and hesitate. They look out into the farm fields in the wrong direction. They don't see Marco! *Hey, he's over here, guys! Over here, by the Bixbys!* But the mysterious dark agents do not hear me, even though I'm the author. Rats!

Next time I'll have to give them super-hearing powers. So Marco makes his getaway. Oh no.

But guess what?

Marco didn't count on tangling with the Bixby boys. Ha! As he jukes through the patch, a small boy's leg darts out from behind a particularly large pumpkin, about shin-high on the escaping felon.

"*Aaaaaaaaaahhhh!*" screams Marco.

By the house, the six dark agents turn their heads in his direction.

Marco falls in a heap, slamming his forehead into a big, wet, ripe pumpkin. When he struggles back to his feet, the pumpkin is lodged on his head. He staggers a few steps, tearing madly at the pumpkin. Finally he rips it off and starts running again, wiping pumpkin guts from his eyes and mouth.

Jake, in a crouch, slithers behind him. Then he executes a perfect ankle-high tackle. Marco and Jake roll over and over. Finally Marco kicks his legs out of Jake's grasp and spins to look at the boy.

"You!" he says.

"Yes, me," says Jake, grinning coldly.

"I'll get you, Bixby!" snarls Marco. "If it's the last thing I do."

"Yeah, well, be sure to send us postcards from C Block," snarls Jake right back.

Lucas pops up from the patch and whispers, "Jake! They're coming!"

The sound of a dozen feet crunching pumpkins can be heard nearby. Jake quickly belly-crawls into nearby weeds as Marco struggles to his feet and tries to run again. But before he can take three steps, the dark agents descend upon him like a pack of wolves.

Let the howling begin!

Three guys pin Marco to the ground. A fourth slaps

handcuffs on his wrists. A fifth shackles his legs. And the last guy, who seems to be the leader, hovers over the prisoner's face.

He says: "Punk, you stand accused of attacking the information infrastructure of the United States of America. You have the right to remain silent, punk. You, punk, have the right to—"

Jake and Lucas lay frozen, not more than thirty feet away.

In their ears, they hear Cyril say, Hey, guys, looks like there's some activity in the pumpkin patch. You might want to check it out.

The Bixby boys give each other a look.

Then they grin.

And they give each other the secret Bixby handshake, one that legend says originated with the very first Bixby, Urdmak of Abyssinia, sometime back in the sixth century B.C.

THE SUNDAY AFTER

Sundays are always perfect in the Bixby home at 44444 Agincourt Drive.

No school, no soccer tournaments, no piano or saxophone lessons (Jake plays tenor, Lucas alto), no tae kwon do classes, no meetings of Junior Leaders of Future American Excellence in Commerce, no chores or schedules or homework. Just free time, together. Every Bixby finds this lack of structure relaxing—with the possible exception of Mrs. Bixby.

"Let's make brownies!" she suggests that Sunday.

"Oh please, no," says Mr. Bixby, looking up in alarm from his newspaper.

"I have this *excellent* new recipe," says Mrs. Bixby brightly, holding up five or six sheets of paper. "I found it yesterday on the Internet. We could execute it together, as a family!"

Across the room Jake and Lucas play chess on one of those theme chess sets, where all of the pieces depict guys from *Star Wars* or *Lord of the Rings* or whatever. In this case, their marble chess pieces are all shaped like famous accountants.

Lucas whispers, "Man, not another brownie project."

Jake nods. "I wonder if this one will have flowcharts again."

"It takes, like, twelve hours just to assemble the ingredients," says Lucas.

"Maybe we can skip some steps," says Jake.

The boys burst out laughing because everyone knows "skipping steps" is not an option in Mrs. Bixby's way of life.

"How did you get online yesterday?" says Mr. Bixby to his lovely wife. "I thought the Internet was all messed up."

"Well," says Mrs. Bixby, "the attack only slowed things a bit."

"What attack?"

"Don't you read the newspapers?"

"No," says Mr. Bixby, turning a page of his newspaper.

"Didn't you read about the attack on the Internet?" she says to her husband. "The coordinated attack? On all thirteen servers of the Internet? But it failed, for some unknown reason?"

"No."

"You didn't?"

"No, I didn't."

"Then how did you know the Internet was messed up?"

"You told me," says Mr. Bixby.

"But you didn't *read* about it?"

"No, I didn't."

"Why not?"

"I'm not sure." Actually, Mr. Bixby refuses to read anything but the sports section on weekends. "Say, look at this," he says, trying to change the subject. "Ha! No more Saturday soccer atrocities."

Both brothers perk up.

"Why?" says Jake.

Their mother says, "Wouldn't you boys like to help me make some nice, warm—"

"'Officials of the Carrolton Crush Soccer Corporation,'" interrupts Mr. Bixby, reading very loudly, "'announced yesterday that its club teams will compete next spring in a newly formed traveling league.'"

"Wow!" says Jake.

Mr. Bixby continues reading. "'At the weekly Crush press conference, club president Ronaldo Beckham unveiled plans for the new Super Division. Other league members will include teams from the surrounding tricounty area,'" he said, "'plus England and Germany.'"

Suddenly Mr. Bixby's cell phone rings.

He looks at it.

After another ring, Mr. Bixby hesitates . . . then drops his paper and lunges for the phone.

Mrs. Bixby dives across the room in one impressive leap. *"No business calls on Sunday!"* she shrieks.

She falls on the phone just as Mr. Bixby seizes it.

As the struggle ensues, the boys step out onto the front porch.

Ah, what a beautiful day in Carrolton! Autumn trees seem to be splashed like paint against the blue sky. Jake and Lucas see Cyril's big feet flopping up the street. His head is down, and he appears to be thinking deeply—so deeply that he doesn't see the Bixby mailbox until it's a little too late.

"Oooooo," says Jake, watching.

"That's gotta hurt," says Lucas.

But Cyril bounces back to his feet pretty quickly and jogs up to the Bixby porch.

"Yo, bro," he says, raising a fist.

Jake nods and points. He says, "'Sgoing down, dog?"

Cyril just shakes his head.

Jake says, "Dude, something's on your mind."

Cyril manages a half smile. "Yeah, well, I guess spies have a lot to think about."

"You been over to Stoneship today?" asks Jake.

"No."

"Really?"

Cyril gives him a look. "I'm never going there alone again," he says.

"Don't blame you," says Jake.

They all stare out into the amazing perfection of Carrolton's afternoon colors. Looking at the red and gold trees, the adventure of the previous few days seems unreal, almost like a dark, foggy dream. *Did we really see the things we saw? Are mysterious men really drifting through the night in black cars, grabbing bad guys and disappearing like smoke?*

Is there a scary Dark Man lurking in Stoneship Woods?

Are we really spies?

When the three boys step back into the house, the living room is torn to shreds.

Mr. Bixby lies in a crumpled heap on the floor while Mrs. Bixby beats on his cell phone with a ball-peen hammer. Okay, I'm just kidding, everything is normal, actually, although Mr. Bixby is tickling Mrs. Bixby, who shrieks with insane laughter.

"Give me that phone!" yells Mr. Bixby, grinning like a maniac.

"No! Never!" howls Mrs. Bixby.

Mr. Bixby tries to pry the phone out of her hands. She chucks it across the floor, under the sofa. He tries to crawl after it, but Mrs. Bixby gets him pretty good by the ankle, and won't let go. Laughing hysterically, they grapple like wild beasts.

"Interesting," says Cyril, watching.

"Maybe we should go upstairs," says Lucas.

"Yes, let's," says Jake, climbing the steps.

When they enter the Bixby boys' bedroom—like all really good brothers, they share a room—Lexi is sitting at Jake's computer, playing a massively multiplayer online game. Lucas almost asks how Lexi got in, but then notices the open window.

"You climbing fool," says Lucas, slapping Lexi's hand.

"Hey, isn't that Warfire: Hammer of Gradnok?" says Cyril.

"Yes," says Lexi.

"How is it?"

Lexi grabs the mouse, slays a few things on-screen, and then turns to Cyril. "I'm glad we saved the Internet," she says.

"That good, eh?"

"It's the best game ever."

As Cyril and Lucas lean over Lexi's shoulders to check out Warfire, Jake sits on his bed. He lies back on the pillow, and tucks his hands behind his head. He stares up at the World War II fighter models hanging from the ceiling. Jake's had a lot on his mind the past twenty-four hours. The first adventure of Team Spy Gear has triggered some deep thoughts and feelings.

For example: Jake feels a very satisfying sense of loyalty to his brother, his buddies, his parents, and his community.

He searches his memory of the Marco incident and remembers when this growing feeling of loyalty became most intense—almost overwhelming, in fact. It was at the very moment when Jake first understood the nature of Marco's nasty scheme . . . and he suddenly realized the *harm* it could cause.

Needless harm . . . to innocent people.

People in Carrolton, and elsewhere too.

At that moment—when Jake realized that—he felt he could do almost anything to stop bad guys like Marco and his fellow plotters.

Speaking of which . . .

"So guys," says Jake. "Who's Viper?"

Conversation stops. They all turn to him.

Suddenly Lexi slaps her own cheek. "Yeah, *I'm* a moron," she says.

Lucas smiles at his short friend. "Why, dude?"

Lexi pulls a 2-Hour Photo packet out of her pocket. She says, "I picked these up today." She extracts a photograph and slaps it down on the desk.

Lucas leans down to look. "Whoa, check it out," he says. "Jake, it's the Viper e-mail to Marco. The one that Lexi photographed with her Spy Camera."

All four kids squint closely. The e-mail window is small, so it cuts off the top section of the message from Viper. It reads:

Opposition has been, shall we say, eliminated. As for detection, don't worry—your part in the plan is smaller than you think. Tonight is just a test. If you and your motley crew perform well, a much more important and remunerative role might be in the works as we acquire the influence we seek in higher circles.

Remember to wipe your drive clean of this and all other correspondence immediately. Nothing must be traced to me. I cannot stress this enough. A mistake of that sort would be very costly . . . perhaps even fatal.

Viper

Jake sits back on the bed and looks up at Cyril. He says, "What does it mean?"

Cyril rubs his shock of hair. "I don't know," he says. "But it sounds, well—"

"Bad," says Lexi.

Cyril looks at her. "Good word, Houdini," he says. "Yes, it's definitely that."

Lucas keeps staring at the cryptic message. Jake looks over at his little brother.

"What do you think?" asks Jake.

Lucas looks up. He says, "It sounds, like . . . *bigger*, doesn't it?"

"Bigger?"

"Yeah, bigger."

"Bigger than what?"

"Bigger than just Marco and a bunch of lowly hacker geeks, for one thing," says Lucas, bouncing nervously and pounding a fist into his other hand. "Maybe even—well, this sounds funny, but—" He pauses and takes a breath.

"Maybe even what?"

"Well, maybe even bigger than a crazy plan to crash the entire Internet."

"That's pretty big."

"Yeah," nods Lucas. "And then there's *this* thing." He reaches down under his bed and pulls out the Omega Link. "This guy comes through in the clutch, man. But how? Is it artificially intelligent? Or . . . is someone, somewhere, sending stuff to it? I mean, is someone *communicating* with us?"

"Good question," says Jake.

Lucas shakes the Omega Link, then holds it up to his ear. No sound. Nothing. He looks at it. The screen is completely blank. They all stand silent for a few moments, looking at the odd gadget. Then Cyril picks up the e-mail photograph.

"Here's another weird thought," he says.

Jake says, "Okay, we're ready."

Cyril looks at Jake. "The Dark Man in the warehouse," he says.

"Yeah?"

"He was *very* scary."

"I'll bet he was."

"But he didn't touch me, man."

Jake nods.

Cyril looks at the other kids. "And, well, here's where I get to the weird part—when I actually *saw* him down below through the Spy Night Scope, he was standing there, sort of looking up at me. And, I swear, I think he was, like, doing a little wave thing." He waves his hand, quickly. "Like this."

"He waved at you?"

"Not exactly," says Cyril. "It seemed more like a signal."

Jake leans forward, keenly interested. He says, "What do you think it means, this signal?"

Cyril gets a wry look. "Ah, I don't know," he says.

Jake grins and says, "Come on, man. I know you're thinking something."

Cyril's hair bobs slightly. "Okay," he says. "I've been thinking about this all day. And I think it was like he was saying, 'It's okay, man. I got it covered.' Or something like that."

"Why do you think that?"

"Well," says Cyril. "*Somebody* called in the black cars on poor Marco, right?"

Lexi freezes. "What if those were Viper's men?"

"Couldn't be!" says Lucas excitedly.

"Why not?" asks Jake.

Lucas jumps up and down, poking his brother's shoulder. "Dude, remember what they did when they grabbed Marco?" he says.

Jake's eyes brighten. "Oh yeah," he says.

"What?" says Cyril. "What'd they do?"

"They read him his Miranda rights."

"I don't think bad guys do that," chuckles Lucas. "My guess is the dark agents were some sort of official law enforcement group." He nods. "Which one, though? A secret one, maybe?"

Okay, there's a lot to ponder here.

The four friends hash over the facts of the case for a good hour. Everyone has ideas. Everyone has theories. Everyone agrees that Marco is merely a pawn in a bigger game, and that maybe Viper is the chess master. But who is he? What does he want? Is he some evil mastermind? What is Viper's ultimate target?

Wow!

Precise calculations are hard to come by, but some data suggests that each kid's brain expands by approximately .37801 percent just because of all the stimulating thought in the room.

Finally it's too much. The gang can't think anymore. Silence falls.

And then Jake gets an idea.

"Hey, guys," says Jake, with a gleam in his eyes.

"What?"

"What, man?"

"What, bro?"

The other three watch Jake expectantly. He grins his famous grin. The others can't help it—they grin back. They are best buddies. They are a family, in fact—a family of *spies*, no less. Yeah! *That's* who they are. Spies, by gosh! They are Team Spy Gear. And hey, don't you forget it, pal.

Jake stands up on his bed.

He raises his finger. He pauses for effect.

That boy is on the verge of a momentous declaration, I tell you.

Finally he says:

"Let's go make some brownies."

After a moment more of stunned silence, the others explode in a whoop of approval. *Woo-hoo!* Then the best spy dudes in Carrolton (and maybe the world) thunder down the stairs.

Evil and mystery are out there, for sure. A Viper lurks in his nest, somewhere.

But that can wait.

Today, Sunday, is a day for making brownies—perhaps even the most complicated ones ever made.